Give Yourself Goosebumps

The Knight in Screaming Armour

R. L. Stine

Scholastic Children's Books
Commonwealth House, 1–19 New Oxford Street, London WC1A 1NU, UK
a division of Scholastic Ltd
London ~ New York ~ Toronto ~ Sydney ~ Auckland

First published in the USA by Scholastic Inc., 1996
First published in the UK by Scholastic Ltd, 1998

Copyright © Parachute Press, Inc., 1996
GOOSEBUMPS is a trademark of Parachute Press, Inc.

ISBN 0 590 12288 6

Typeset by Rowland Phototypesetting Ltd, Bury St Edmunds, Suffolk
Printed by Cox & Wyman Ltd, Reading, Berks.

10 9 8 7 6 5 4 3 2 1

BEWARE!!
DO NOT READ THIS
BOOK FROM BEGINNING TO END!

Prepare yourself to meet the Knight in Screaming Armour!

Your cousins are coming to visit you from England. They're bringing something with them. A little surprise . . .

It's an old suit of armour from your uncle's collection. It has a really cool battleaxe and a shield. And it has something else too—orders to destroy you!

You see, there's an ancient curse that was placed upon your family and the knight is here to deliver it! And that's not all—a ghastly-looking gardener with three heads, Mud Slinging monsters made of goo, and some very nasty sheep are all coming your way!

This scary adventure is all about you. You decide what will happen. And you decide how terrifying the scares will be.

Start on page 1. Then follow the instructions at the bottom of each page. You make the choices.

If you make the right choices, you will defeat the Knight in Screaming Armour and escape its horrible curse. If you make the wrong choice . . . BEWARE!

SO TAKE A DEEP BREATH. CROSS YOUR FINGERS. AND TURN TO PAGE 1 NOW TO *GIVE YOURSELF GOOSEBUMPS!*

READER BEWARE—
YOU CHOOSE THE SCARE!

Look for more
GIVE YOURSELF GOOSEBUMPS adventures
from R. L. STINE:

"Pip-pip! Ta-ta! Jolly good! Tallyho and all that rot!" your dad exclaims.

"Da-a-a-d!" you plead. "Pleeeeeeease!"

"So sorry," he apologizes in his best British accent. "We just want your cousins to feel quite at home now, don't we? It's not every day we have visitors from England. It's been over a year since we've seen them. Jolly good! Ta-ta! Pip-pip!" your dad says again.

"Yes," your mum adds. "Your Uncle Will is giving lectures at several important American museums. So Kip and Abbey will be staying with us for a whole week. Isn't that terrific!"

You only half agree. Kip Saxton is your age. Sometimes he complains too much. But mostly, he's a pretty cool kid. His fifteen-year-old sister is another story. "Abbey acts like she's queen of the world," you say. "She can be a royal pain!"

"Oh, you'll have fun," your dad assures you. "Uncle Will says Kip and Abbey are bringing a big surprise with them!"

"A surprise?" you ask. "What surprise?"

Go to PAGE 2.

2

Before your dad can say another word about the surprise, the doorbell rings.

"They're here!" your mum calls from the front hall. She opens the door as the airport shuttle van pulls away. Your cousins are standing in the doorway. "You haven't changed a bit!" your mum declares as she hugs Abbey and Kip.

"I hope that's not true," you mutter. Your tall blonde cousin is already staring past you and into the mirror behind you. "Hi," you manage to say to her.

Abbey primps her long golden curls before she answers. "Oh, hi," she says as she pats her hair about a hundred times.

"Still the same old Abbey," you have to admit.

"Forget her," someone says, laughing. It's Kip. "Can you give me a hand? We've got more stuff to bring in." Your sandy-haired cousin moves back out on to the front step and points to two huge wooden crates. The crates are taller than your dad.

"What the—?" you start to say.

"Artifacts!" your dad chimes in. "Uncle Will is coming here next week to lecture at the Medieval Museum in the town. I told him we'd store some exhibits here until he arrives. But I never expected anything this big! These crates will have to go in the garage."

"What's in the crates anyway?" you ask Kip.

Go to PAGE 3.

"Two suits of armour," Kip says. "That's what's in the crates. They're really old. From the fifteenth century. We call one of them the Evil Knight. It's been with the Saxton family forever. The other suit was Sir Edmund Saxton's. He's our great-great-great-great- . . . well, you get the picture."

The crates are on wheels. You, Kip, Abbey and your dad pull them down the driveway to the garage behind your house. You notice a label on one of the crates.

"Hey, look at this," you cry. You read the label aloud:

> *"Beware this Dark and Evil Knight*
> *Cursed still from long ago.*
> *Until a Good Knight fights for right*
> *This Knight brings misery and woe.*

That's kind of spooky," you add.

"No! Don't read that out loud," Kip cautions too late. "It's an evil curse on the whole Saxton family!"

"A curse?" You laugh. "You don't believe in curses, do you?"

"Sure I do. And so should you if you know what's good for you," Kip whispers. "I suppose you've never heard the tale."

Listen to the tale on PAGE 4.

4

"The tale? What tale?" you ask.

"The legend of the Curse of the Knight in Screaming Armour!" Kip answers. "Years ago an evil sorceress got angry with the King's best knight, Sir Edmund Saxton. You know, our ancestor? He'd killed her favourite dragon, or something. Anyway, she put a curse on him— the Curse of the Knight in Screaming Armour!

"She made a special suit of armour and sent it to him as a gift. The armour was haunted. It held the spirit of an evil knight. That night, horrible screams and cries were heard from Saxton castle. In the morning, Sir Edmund and all of his family had been killed!"

Kip's eyes grow wide as he goes on. "All of his family was dead except one son. He had been out hunting. Anyway, he kept the armour. He was too scared to throw it away!"

The four of you arrive at the garage and your dad reaches down to open the door.

"This is that armour. Family legend has it that one day it will wake up again. Thirsty for Saxton blood. Then it will destroy all that is good! Unless a brave and noble Saxton can defeat it. It *has* to be a member of the Saxton family."

"Ha!" you laugh. "I'm related to you, so I'm a Saxton. What's an Evil Knight's suit of armour going to do to me?"

Get your answer on PAGE 96.

The hands on the silvery-green clock move too easily when you turn them backwards. By mistake you turn them right past one o'clock, past midnight, past eleven, ten, nine, eight . . . In fact, they're turning backwards on their own. As the clock hands start to speed round the dial, Kip and Abbey start laughing.

"What's so funny?" you ask.

"Your face is changing!" Abbey giggles and points to Kip. "You're starting to look chubby. Like a chubby little baby!"

"And Abbey's getting shorter!" Kip laughs. "Look at her clothes. They're huge on her!" Now Kip is rolling on the floor laughing. When he tries to stand up, he can't. All he can do is crawl!

With each turn of the clock's hands you, Kip and Abbey grow younger. "I want my mama!" Abbey sobs. "I want my teddy bear!"

"I want my bottle!" Kip sniffs.

Now they're both crying like two hungry babies. Your mind is racing. You can't take your eyes off them and the fantastic transformation taking place before you. But when you happen to glance down, what you see horrifies you—two pudgy little hands holding on to a spinning clock dial! You must do something before it's too late! Or too early! Before the clock takes you back to a time *before you were born*!

Quick! Before your hands are too tiny to turn the page, turn to PAGE 44.

6

The old woman has aged and shrivelled up. You act as fast as your withered hand will move.

Using all the strength left in your wretched old bones, you move the black hands of the hot-pink clock backwards. There is a rushing of wind. It feels like rain against your parched old skin. Slowly you, Abbey and Kip get younger again. You stare at Abbey's dried-apple face. It puffs and tightens until it is once again fresh and young. Kip and you are both back to your usual selves.

When it's all over, you turn your attention to what's left of the Keeper of All Times. She's nothing but a piece of parchment on the floor. You pick it up and read:

"Time goes by and comes again,
Time stops and goes and stops and then . . .

It's another clue!" you shout.

"Okay, smarty-pants, then what does it mean?" You can tell Abbey is really curious.

"Well," you think aloud, "the pink clock turned time forwards. I bet the silvery-green clock turns time backwards. But what I can't figure out is what this orange clock does . . ."

Turn to PAGE 68.

You slam yourself against the door at the back of the roomful of clocks. It won't budge.

"Push harder!" Abbey yells over the deafening sounds of all the clocks. The three of you lean your shoulders into the door and push. One more hard shove and it springs open!

"Yaaaaaaaaaaaaaaaaaaaayyyyyyyyyyyy!!!" you all cheer together as you fall through the doorway and on to a long spiral slide. You hang on to each other. You're speeding down a massive slide to a deeper, darker place. It's as if you're on a roller coaster into the unknown . . .

"Wheeeeeeeeeeeeeeeeeeeeeeeeeeeeeeeeeeeeeeeeeeeeeeeeeee
eeeeeeeeeeeeeeeeeeeeeeeeeeeeeeeeeeeeeeeeeeeeeeeeee
eeeeeeeeeeeeeeeeeeeeeeeeeeeeeeeeeeeeeeeeeeeeee
eeeeeeeeeeeeeeeeeeeeeeeeeeeeeeeee
eeeeeeeeee . . ."

Slide on down to PAGE 69.

All this head-switching business is giving you a royal headache. And you still have the head of a queen! This can't be the way it all ends. You as a queen, Abbey as you, and Kip as a drooling gargoyle.

You think of the missing armour. The suit of Sir Edmund, the Good Knight. You think of the pieces of parchment you found—the clues along the way. Surely, you're destined to find the armour. What did the parchment say? *Before the break of day brings light, One Good shall fight one Evil Knight.* If not, the Evil Knight will destroy all that is good. That can't be good for you.

RRRIIIINNGGG! Somewhere, you hear a clock strike. It sounds like it's far away. And what's that tickling your belly?

The clock! It's not far away, it's under your sweatshirt! You pull it out and look at it. Both the green and the pink clocks say 6:00 a.m. The sun will be up soon!

As if on cue, all the heads in the room start screaming! And this room has a lot of heads! Even Abbey and Kip, or what's left of them, scream. *Before the break of day brings light ...* you think. You're running out of time! Already you can hear the chilling laughter of the Knight in Screaming Armour closing in!!

If time is on your side, turn to PAGE 25.
If time is against you, turn to PAGE 14.

"All right, all right, enough's enough. This is getting a little too weird for me," you say. "It's time to call the police."

"Chicken," Abbey mocks you. You just ignore her.

"But only a Saxton can break the curse," Kip reminds you. "The police won't be able to do anything."

"Well, I for one am willing to let them try."

You shove the GOOD KNIGHT crate door closed and start buckling the leather straps. Then the loudest scream of the night fills the air. Followed by a crunching noise. You whirl round to look, and your heart almost leaps out of your chest.

The Evil Knight has crashed one of his armoured arms through the other wooden crate. A thick-fingered, steely, armoured glove gleams in the dim light. And it's gripping Abbey's slender neck.

Hurry! Run to PAGE 83.

You squeal in horror and shiver as the snake's clammy body wriggles down your arm and drops to the floor. Then you notice a familiar-looking piece of parchment speared on one of its poisonous fangs!

You almost can't believe it. You know you have to get that parchment. Carefully, you reach down. Somehow, you manage to pluck it off without getting bitten. The snake slithers away.

"Hey, look what I've found!" you shout and glance round for Kip and Abbey. But you're all alone. Well, not quite alone.

A chorus of hideous snarls, moans and cackles answers you. You try to ignore it and read what's on the parchment. But it's much too dark.

You need more light.

The lighting is better on PAGE 36.

You can't trust your own head to keep Kip from being buried by a regiment of rolling soldier heads. Instead, you gaze round the room for someone more intelligent. In the furthest corner of the room you spy one lonely head resting on the highest shelf.

Aha, you think. *It's on the highest shelf. It probably has the highest IQ.*

You dash to the corner. Using the other shelves as steps, you climb until you are even with the highest head-stand. Its face is turned away from you. But before you can touch the head to turn it, it starts to turn on its own! It slowly spins and meets you eye to eye.

IT'S THE HEAD OF THE EVIL KNIGHT!!!!!!!!

"AAAAaaahhhh!" you scream in terror as your heads are instantly switched.

It is a bone-chilling scream.

It is the scream of the Knight in Screaming Armour!

And that's YOU!

THE END

Abbey sputters as she wipes globs of thick brown mud from her mouth and eyes. Now she sees what you and Kip have already seen. The walls are *alive!*

Short, square-bodied mud beasts step out from the dirt-coloured walls. They start flinging handfuls of thick oozing mud.

"THWAAAAPPP!" A glob catches you in the ear.

"TCHWAAANNK!" A fistful of the well-packed mud covers Kip's sandy hair and slides down over his eyes.

"What's happening?!" Kip cries.

"THWAAAAAPPP!" comes the answer in the form of a special delivery mud-o-gram.

The oozy mud in your ear starts to harden and crack. You rip at it with your fingers. *"SKOOOOOIIIINSH!"* You're caught in the stomach by another mud glob. It hardens on contact. It makes it difficult to breathe. You've got to get out of here!

The Mud Slingers gang up on Abbey. They swing their gorilla arms and pack more solid mud-balls to throw at her. "Aaahhhh!" Abbey sobs as one hard mud-ball nails her on the knee. "Why me? Why me?" she screams, clutching her bashed knee.

Go to PAGE 22.

You pull the covers up over your head and try to go back to sleep. After all, Abbey had said the story about the knight wasn't true.

You can't sleep. There's another shriek. And another. The screaming grows louder and more chilling. And it's getting closer! That last one seemed to come from just outside your door!

Wait. What's that? Something is moving at the foot of your bed. You strain your eyes to see in the darkness. You immediately wish you hadn't. A shadowy figure seems to hover at your feet, ready to attack. "It's the knight!" you shout as you spring up in bed.

Quick! Turn to PAGE 67.

14

The clock you've taken out from under your sweatshirt is ringing wildly! Louder and louder. The heads on the shelves stare out at you. Rows and rows of heads with gaping mouths. Screaming at you. Your heart knocks against your ribs.

Your pulse begins to race.

"Help!" you shout. But no one hears you over the shrieking heads. You shut your eyes, but they're not really yours. Your head still looks like a queen.

Is your time up?

That's it, you think. *Time. It strikes you, you've got to use the clock!*

You look closely at the three-faced clock. "The orange clock face," you mutter to yourself. "This must be the time to use it." You touch it with your finger. It's the last thing you do.

The green clock face moves time backwards. The pink one moves it forwards. The orange one stops it, cold.

You always wondered how it would end. And now you know. Just like this, for ever and ever. Looks like time's run out for you!

THE END

You jump back and grab your cheek where the claws scraped you. You feel a large welt. You turn away from Abbey and grope along the wall until you find the light switch. *CLICK.* One bare bulb hanging from the ceiling floods the garage with a dim light. Suddenly, everything goes quiet.

Now you see it. The monster blocking your escape route is a lawn mower.

The sharp-nailed fingers that raked across your cheek are exactly what they felt like—a garden rake.

And the snake coiled so tightly around Abbey's legs is a hose.

"I knew it all along," Abbey says as she throws the hose aside. "This whole thing is ridiculous!"

But it isn't over yet. *"Eeeeeeeeeeee!"* Whatever's in the EVIL KNIGHT crate demands your attention. The crate lurches forward, knocking Abbey to the ground.

Help Abbey on PAGE 131.

16

The Evil Knight's head is a steaming hunk of black metal. A sparkling medallion hangs round his neck. Something about his medallion holds your gaze. You can't stop looking at it! With you standing there helpless before him, the Evil Knight raises his heavy sword and ... and ...

He brings it down and slashes open the back of the crate behind him. The wood shatters like ice.

"IN THE LAND OF SAXTONS YOU SHALL BE DESTROYED!" His voice booms over you. You shiver. He glances back at you and then disappears through the new opening.

You're not sure how long you stand there in shock. The next thing you know, Abbey and Kip are standing next to you.

"D-d-d-did you see th-th-that?" you stammer.

"Yeah, no big deal." Abbey tries to sound cool.

"Look!" Kip exclaims. "This hole in the back of the crate—there are hills in it!"

"Yeah, right! What's that mean?" Abbey huffs.

But he's *right*. You peer through the hole. You see emerald-green hills and a pale blue sky. You feel wind against your face. You feel yourself drawn to the scene. Like you were to the medallion.

"We'd better go through," you say without taking your eyes off the scene before you. "If not, we'll never break this curse thing." You push aside the splinters and step through ...

Step out of the crate on PAGE 119.

A pair of mud-slimed arms push out of the wall. They wrap around you, holding you in place. Mud-balls fly at you faster and harder.

"*SPLAT!*" Your head is covered.

"*WHACK!*" Your arms are covered.

"*TCHOOOWOK! KAAACHINK! SWAAAK!*" The thick sludge mud covers all of you. Your mud-encased body stiffens as the ooze hardens.

Welcome to the dirty world of the Evil Knight and his army of Mud Slingers. They always fight dirty and they always, always win in

THE END.

"Who are you?" you ask in a cracking voice.

"I am the Keeper of All Times—I decide whose time has come and whose time is past," the prune-faced woman cries. "You are taking too much of my time. Now I must take away all your time. Wither! Dust to Dust! Be Gone!"

Even as she points her spell-casting finger at you, the skin on your arms turns papery thin with instant age. It hangs from your arms like sheets of wet tissue. You're afraid it will tear! You must stop this curse of aging before you all end up as a pile of dust on the floor.

"Help us?" you cry in your crackly voice.

"Ha!" cackles the old woman. "Help you? After what you have done to me? Wither! Fade! Be Gone!"

"The clock!" Kip whispers. "Use the clock!"

While there's still TIME, turn to PAGE 107.

"SCREEEEEEEEEEEEEEEEE!"   Another shriek fills the night. Kip and Abbey are as wide-awake as you are. The piercing screams draw the three of you together at your bedside. You grab each of your cousins by the hand.

"We have to go out to the garage and investigate," you declare. "We have to find out what's out there."

Another scream pierces the air. Abbey forgets how much cooler than you she is for a moment and clutches one of your arms. Kip grabs your other one. You grab a torch from your desk and make your way out into the night. You pull your cousins along behind you. Eventually, you come to the garage door. You pause a moment and listen to the screams.

"Well, here goes," you say. You reach down, grab the handle, and lift it open.

Quick, turn to PAGE 113.

You wake up. The last thing you remember is finding the piece of parchment that said, "Before the break of day brings light, One Good shall fight one Evil Knight . . ."

You rub your eyes to clear the sleep out of them. You see Kip and Abbey. But you're not in the garage any more.

A bare bulb hangs from a wire in the ceiling. It casts a sickly yellow-brown tint over the enormous cavern of a room. The walls and ceiling are the colour of mud.

"At least we're still together," you say.

"But where are we?" Abbey asks. "Hello! Is anybody there?"

No one answers.

The air is musty and stale. It reminds you of something. In fact, it's just like the air in the old museum you went to on a school field trip last month. Then you see the muddy sign on one wall: THE MEDIEVAL MUSEUM.

"Hey!" you shout excitedly. "We're in the town centre. This is the museum where your dad is supposed to speak next week!"

"Museum?" Abbey shoots back at you. "There's nothing here at—" Her mouth is open when a great splat of mud hits her right in the face! *THWACK!*

Follow this dirty business to PAGE 12.

"WELCOME TO YOUR DOOM!" The Evil Knight roars as Kip and Abbey step into the darkness.

"Go back!" you shout to your cousins. "I've found the last piece of the puzzle. It said, 'When Evil fights and Good defends, the curse of Screaming Armour ends.' But it's no use. There's too much evil in this place. Go back!"

"We can't go back!" Kip shouts. "The door closed behind us."

"We can't win!" you yell. "Without Sir Edmund's armour we don't have a chance!"

"We have to earn the armour!" Kip cries. "We have to show that we are brave enough to wear the armour of a knight. That's the way the curse is written!"

You know Kip is right. Only the bravest become knights. And you don't know about Kip and Abbey, but you aren't feeling too brave at the moment.

Turn to PAGE 114.

You want to help Abbey. She's clutching her knee in agony. But before you can comfort Abbey, you've got a new problem of your own.

Another Mud Slinger slides out of the wall and stomps towards you. The broad, blubber-lipped creature is so close you can smell his oozy stench. You cough and sputter.

Disgusting streams of muddy liquid ooze from his yellow eyes and flaring nostrils. Right behind him is another Mud Slinger. And another. And another!

If you feel hopelessly walled-in by the mound of menacing Mud Slingers, turn to PAGE 55.

If you pull yourself out of this mud mess, turn to PAGE 86.

There's no way you're waiting round to see what's got those hedgehogs spooked. There's no telling when the Evil Knight might show up again. Back into the hedges it is.

"Anything's better than facing that horrible hunk of screaming armoured junk!" you say. But the hedges have already grown over the hole you broke through.

You try pulling the thick bushes apart. Your fingers are scraped and swollen. "It's no use trying to pull the hedge apart, we'll have to try smashing through again."

You link arms and turn your backs to the high hedges. "On the count of three we go!" you say. "One, two, three!" All together you crash back through the hedge.

You land with a *THUD*. The ground is awfully hard. You look round and discover the strangest thing yet.

Turn to PAGE 112.

24

The electrical charge fuses you, Kip and Abbey together. You can't pull yourselves apart.

With the room now the size of a walk-in wardrobe and getting smaller by the second, you can barely move. Each movement causes a shower of new sparks to rain down over your heads. You can't even stretch your arms up enough to shelter yourselves from the biting, burning sparks.

All you can do is wait. You hope the sparks and the deadly charge surging through you will stop before it's too late.

Turn to PAGE 91.

Time is on your side. Without even thinking, you turn back the hands on the silvery-green clock face. You're careful not to move them too much.

Time goes in reverse. But only a few minutes. You watch in fascination as the last few minutes are rewound like on a VCR. Heads pop on and off until you're all back to normal and you're back where you started again. Your heads are spinning. Your ears are ringing. And your noses are pressed up against a wall of glass.

You see two buttons. One says HEADS and the other says TALES. You reach into your pocket and take out a coin.

Toss a coin to help you decide which button to push. If you push HEADS, turn to PAGE 103. If you push TALES, turn to PAGE 26.

26

You push the button that says TALES.

Immediately the three of you are back in your house about to hear one of the greatest *tales* ever told.

Go to PAGE 4.

Hedges are exploding out of the ground fully grown. They're spreading towards you with amazing speed. You're no match for them. They burst past you, blocking your path. You try to stop short. But not fast enough to avoid a faceful of prickles. Kip and Abbey, too.

You start to run the other way. But you don't get far before you come up against another wall of hedge!

It doesn't seem to matter which way you turn. Any open path is instantly blocked by a solid wall of high bramble bushes.

Prickly branches grab at you as you run past! You shake them off and keep on running. You have to get out of here! The walls around you grow higher and higher, cutting the sky into lines of blue.

The three of you race in every direction. But it's no use. You stop for a second to catch your breath.

The ground beneath you starts to rumble and shake. "Aaaaaaahhhhhhh!" you scream. You can imagine the hedge about to explode through the ground and up through your body! You brace yourself.

But then it stops. It's quiet again. Except for Kip.

"We're trapped!" he bellows. "What do we do now?"

Try to escape on PAGE 78.

"Where are you going?" Kip asks you as you carefully step off your rocking rock and on to his.

"Look up there," you say. You point to the gleaming object. "I have a feeling whatever is up there is something we need. I don't know why, but I have to find out what it is. I'm going up to get it."

"I'll come with you!" Kip volunteers.

"Stop right there," Abbey orders. "Don't take another step. You're not leaving *me* alone!"

"Oh yeah. Abbey's afraid of heights," Kip mumbles.

"I'll go by myself," you declare. "You two stay together here." Balancing on all fours, you move up on to the next rock.

You feel as if you're climbing on eggshells. One false move and the rock you're on could crumble away. You would tumble all the way to the bottom. You test each rock before you move to it. It's amazing how many of them have jagged edges! Higher and higher you climb.

Then you see it.

A hand! Sticking up out of the rocks!

Look closer on PAGE 133.

You throw the mud beast to the ground with all your might. *"SSSKWIIISHSH-BOOOOOOM!"* There's an explosion of oozy mud. Mud fills the air. You're thrown to the floor. Everything goes dark.

When you open your eyes, you see the bare bulb hanging down from the ceiling above you. But it's not the bare bulb in the Medieval Museum. It's the one right in your own garage!

"Hahahahahaha . . ." You hear laughter. Your heart skips a beat. Is it the Evil Knight?

You sit up. It's only Kip and Abbey. They're sitting next to you laughing and pointing at you. The two crates stand silent and still. There's nothing strange going on here at all. Except for the fact that you, Kip and Abbey are all safe. There's no trace of mud anywhere. Were the Mud Slingers and the Evil Knight all in your imagination?

"Did you see anything weird a moment ago?" you ask your cousins.

"Not me," Kip says innocently.

"Not I," Abbey corrects him.

"I neither, I suppose," you say.

"Me neither," Abbey corrects you. "Don't you know anything?"

One thing you aren't imagining. Abbey hasn't changed a bit. She always has to have the last word in

THE END.

Your mother always tells you to "use your head". Now's your chance! Quick, before Kip loses his!

It seems that all you have to do to switch your head in this crazy room is stare into the eyes of another. Without a moment to lose, you move in front of Queen Abbey. You look directly into her eyes and . . .

"Guards!" you shout a second later. "Return to your head-stands at once!" Now you are the Queen with the diamond tiara and the guards must obey you!

The rolling heads of the guards reverse their rolling direction immediately. Keeping their formation, they roll back to their head-stands and plant themselves on the shelf. Kip is safe!

All is well. Except for one little problem— Abbey has your head on, you look like a Queen, and Kip is a hideous, snarling gargoyle. Any idea how to fix this mess? Maybe, if you put your heads together, you might come up with something.

*Turn a-**head** to PAGE 8.*

"He's calling your name!" Abbey warns. "He's after you!"

"ABBEY!" calls the deep and dangerous-sounding voice of the Evil Knight. "KIP!" the voice booms again from somewhere in the next room. He calls your name again.

"COME FORWARD!" the Evil Knight commands. Suddenly you feel a tremendous sense of curiosity. What could this Evil Knight possibly have in mind for you? You feel your feet take a step forward.

"Don't do it. Don't go through that door!" Abbey begs you.

"COME FORWARD!" the Evil Knight orders again.

If you can't resist his command, turn to PAGE 128.

If you take Abbey's advice, turn to PAGE 58.

"Let's go to the left," Abbey says, pulling thorns out of her arms. "There's a cottage down the hill. Maybe we can get help there."

"Hello? Am I the only one who thinks there's something weird going on here?" you ask. Abbey and Kip can't hear you. They're already walking across the windy meadow towards the cottage.

"Pixies!" you mumble to yourself. You take off after Kip and Abbey.

You don't get far when you hear a deafening rumble. It sounds like an earthquake! You see bits of turf flying in the air! You turn and look behind you to see . . .

HEDGES! *Killer* hedges. They're growing at an incredible rate. Actually, they're not so much growing as bursting through the earth in jagged lines. Walls of branches and leaves. And it looks as if, yes, they are . . . heading right for you!

It's time to start sprinting again. And there's no use screaming about it, either. Now's the time to MOVE!

Move over to PAGE 27.

"We'll open the Good Knight crate," you decide. You don't want to take any chances. But as soon as you say this, an ear-splitting scream fills the garage. The Evil Knight crate starts rattling again. The armour inside clanks and rumbles and roars.

You cling to Kip. Or is it Abbey? It's hard to tell in the darkness.

The tall Evil Knight crate rocks closer to you. It tips backwards and forwards. Backwards and forwards. If it falls on you, you'll be crushed! You try to pull your cousins out of the way. "Let's get out!" you yell. But you only get a few steps towards the garage door when something blocks your escape route.

"A horrible beast!" Kip cries.

"Aaaahhhh!" Abbey screams as she's jerked away from your side. You accidentally drop your torch and it hits the concrete floor with a smack. "There's something wrapped around my leg!" Abbey wails.

"Abbey!" you shout across to her. You start to move to her side, but you feel sharp claws scrape across your cheek.

Hurry! Go to PAGE 15!

Yes! Now you get it. It's started to make sense. You know you have to act NOW or you'll either be fried or crushed by the walls. The electrical charge flowing through you is so strong you're lit up like a light bulb. Or like an X-ray.

You stare down at your hands. You can see your bones! You dare to glance at Kip and Abbey. You scream in horror when you see them. They are electrified skeletons!

With sparks zapping and zzztttzing every second, you pull the other piece of parchment back out of your pocket. These are the clues, you think. There has to be a way to escape!

> *. . . Before the break of day brings light,*
> *One Good shall fight one Evil Knight.*
> *Beware his deadly charge and feel*
> *That what is NOW is not what's real . . .*

That what is NOW is not what's real. You think harder. That what is NOW is NOT WHAT'S REAL, the words scream in your head. You force yourself to know that what is happening NOW is not real!

Force yourself to PAGE 57.

Your cousins could be in trouble. Kip and Abbey could be turning to stone this very minute!

"Don't move!" you yell down. "I mean DO move if you can. I'm coming down to save you!"

You take one last glance at the shining object. Rock by rock, you backtrack the way you came. It's even harder to move downward, but there's no time to lose! Mostly, you try not to think about what these rocks and boulders used to be!

You set your foot against what used to be someone's shoulder. It jiggles under your weight. And then it flips up! You tumble head first down the rocky slope.

"Ouch! Ooch! Eech! Ouch!" you yelp with each bump. Finally you land with a crash at your cousins' feet.

Turn to PAGE 101 to find out what's happened to them!

The only light bright enough to read by is the firelight of the dragons' breath. You inch yourself closer to that cage and hold out the jagged-edged piece of parchment.

But just as you are ready to start reading, one of the dragons exhales a long ribbon of flame. The fire touches the parchment. It bursts into flame in your hands.

You throw the paper to the ground. Just before the scrap turns to ashes you get one good look at it. You think it said:

> *When Evil fights and Good defends*
> *The curse of Screaming Armour ends.*

"That sounds familiar," you say to yourself.

You remember what Kip told you about the curse: "The Evil Knight will destroy all that is good, unless a brave and noble Saxton can defeat it. It *has* to be a Saxton." Looking round the room you know one thing for sure. The only good thing round here is YOU.

You also happen to be a Saxton.

Can you handle this much evil on your own?

If you want to try it alone, turn to PAGE 40.
If you need help from your cousins, turn to PAGE 84.

"AAAaaaaaaahhhhhhhhhhhhhh!" you scream when your fingers touch metal.

"Wake up!" you hear Kip's voice saying.

"You're screaming!" Abbey shakes your arm. "Wake up!"

Your eyes flutter open. Your hand rests on the cold metal head of a shovel hanging on your garage wall.

"You've been sleepwalking!" Kip says. "We heard you screaming so we ran to your bedroom. You got out of bed, put on a dressing-gown and walked out here to the garage."

"We followed you just to make sure you were all right," Abbey continues. "You walked up to the crates we brought and just stood in front of them for a really long time. It was weird."

"We tried to talk to you, but you didn't hear us. Then you reached your hand out, touched the shovel and started screaming again!" Kip is laughing now because of the look on your face. You're surprised, embarrassed and relieved all at once. Was it really all a crazy dream?

Turn to PAGE 120.

"We have to free the Good Knight," you yell over the screams and the heavy clanking. "Maybe it can help us fight the curse."

"But . . . but . . ." Kip sputters fearfully.

"Just open the thing," Abbey snaps, "and get it over with!"

Your fingers fly over the buckled leather straps that hold the crate closed.

"I've got this strap at the bottom," Kip says moving in next to you. Abbey just watches you work. You and Kip work together to prise open one side of the crate. The clanking is louder than ever as the crate door slams to the floor. You pick up your torch and shine it inside. Abbey is the first to gasp.

Turn to PAGE 50.

The silver key fits perfectly into the lock, but it won't turn. "I don't get it," you say. "This key looks like it should go with this lock."

No luck. You put the key back in your pocket. You step back from the door to search for another way in. As soon as you move away, the door slowly swings open!

"Come in," the voice of a very old man invites from somewhere inside the cottage. "I've been waiting for you."

"Waiting for us?" Abbey stammers. She peers into the darkened doorway. "But I can't see you," Abbey says.

"Come closer," the old man says in a friendly voice. "It's been so long since I had some good company."

The three of you step into the cottage. The door SLAMS behind you!

If the SLAM makes you scream, turn to PAGE 87.

If the SLAM makes you jump, turn to PAGE 105.

You decide you have to face the Knight in Screaming Armour one-on-one. If Kip and Abbey join you in this evil exhibit hall, you may all come to a terrible end. And these are, after all, *your* nightmares.

Just as you decide not to call them, you hear Kip's voice from the doorway. "Don't come in!" you shout back. "You were right. This place is a torture chamber!"

Before you can stop them, Kip and Abbey pass through the doorway and into the hall of horrors. "Stop!" you warn them. But it's too late. They're in.

Turn to PAGE 21.

Kip and Abbey don't notice that you are running out of the dining-hall. They don't care. They reach back to pull their hoods up over their vanishing heads. Now Kip and Abbey are chanting too.

"No bell tolls for us. No bell tolls for us. No bell tolls for us."

You race down a different set of stone stairs. A doorway at the bottom leads out into a courtyard.

Across the yard is a crumbling bell tower. As you run for it, the chanting monks hurry close behind you. They're not going to let you escape. They want you to join them too.

You race up the broken stone steps to the top of the tower. A rotting rope hangs from a black cast-iron bell. There's a kettle full of a bubbling black liquid on the floor.

You reach for the bell rope, and the ghosts stop in their tracks. They hold their thick sleeves up against their hoods—to where their ears would be if they had ears. As terrified as you are of them, they seem frightened of the bell!

If you pull the rope to ring the bell, turn to **PAGE 110.**

If you decide to throw the liquid at them instead, turn to PAGE 73.

Kip decides the right door is the door on the right. The handle turns easily under his hand. He pushes the door open with his shoulder and falls through. You grab Abbey and throw yourself through the opening just in time. The walls grind together behind you. They make a horrible screech like fingernails across a blackboard. You cover your ears in pain but then all is silent.

Or maybe not quite silent. As your ears become accustomed to the quiet you hear something. It's a ticking.

"Tick, tock, tick, tock . . ." you hear.

"Clocks!" Abbey shouts gleefully. "Hundreds of them! And they're all different!" The ticking gives way to *bongs* and *cuckoos* and chimes of all sorts. The walls around you, the ceiling, even the doors of this new room are covered with clocks. Clocks of all shapes and sizes.

A flashing sign on the wall greets you with the words:

TAKE YOUR TIME LEAVING

"What a relief," you say. "At least clocks can't hurt us."

"Right!" Kip agrees. "But with all of them ticking and bonging, gonging and going cuckoo at once it could drive us crazy in no time!"

"Well, that's the one thing there isn't any of here." You laugh. "No time. Time is *all* we've got in this place!"

Go to PAGE 81.

"Awwk! Awwk!" Abbey the Nighthawk squawks through clenched teeth. She carries you off into the night. You only hope she doesn't drop the two of you. She's flying really fast!

Far below you see the bell tower and the crumbled ruins of the monastery. Ahead you see a giant bird's nest resting on a rocky mountaintop. Abbey the Nighthawk hovers over the nest. She opens her mouth and Kip drops. Then she releases her claws and drops you.

You hit the nest hard. Really hard. And before you know it, a thin white shell starts forming up around you. "We're turning into eggs!" you shout to Kip as the shell closes over your head.

But he can't hear you. His shell is already closed over him. He's trapped and so are you. Now all you can do is wait for the time when you will hatch. That could be soon. Or more than likely, it could be never. For you two eggs, it's over easy.

THE END

"Waaah! Waaah!" Abbey and Kip are sitting on the floor in a puddle of tears. And you're not feeling too happy yourself!

Your own hands have shrunk down to two pudgy little baby fists. The square clock now weighs a tonne. You struggle not to let go. If you lose the clock, it's all over! Or maybe it never began. But the clock's as big as you are, now that you're not as big as you were before!

You rest the clock on the floor and crawl right across the silvery-green face. Your breath is coming in gulps now. It's getting harder to see. Your hands are too weak to do the job they must do, but you're a lot smarter than the average baby.

Using your knees, you crawl forward, pushing the hands of the clock slowly along as you go. As you do, minute by minute, Abbey and Kip gradually return to their normal ages.

As for you, you deserve all the credit. Abbey and Kip should really give you a great big hand! Which is what they do.

Two great big hands scoop down and lift you up.

"Look at the little baby," Abbey coos. "Isn't he cute?"

Oh, no! What's happening? You should all be back to normal, right? But Abbey's rocking you in her enormous arms!

This isn't fair, you think! "WAAAAAAAAA-AAAAAAAAAAAAAHHHHHH!"

THE END

"Swim!" you call out to Kip. "Swim for your life!"

"I can't swim!" Kip calls back. His arms are flailing. Then he disappears under a wave.

You swim as fast as you can to where Kip just was. You reach down with your hand and grab his shirt!

"I've got you!" two voices call out at the same time. One voice is yours. The other is the deep and dark voice of the Knight in Screaming Armour!

You hold Kip up by his shirt collar. He's gasping for breath. Evil laughter comes from the shore of this lake. On the shore you see the tall figure of the Evil Knight. A black nighthawk is sitting on his armoured shoulder.

The bird flies off the Evil Knight's shoulder. When she flies over you, the bird turns back into Abbey! She splashes down. "Help!" she cries. "I can't swim either!"

The Evil Knight's laughter echoes across the lake. "I'LL SAVE YOU!" he bellows. "I'LL SAVE YOU ALL . . . FOR ME!"

Before your eyes the Evil Knight multiplies. Now hundreds of Evil Knights surround the lake shore. It's just a matter of time now. You're all washed up!

THE END

46

Aha! You *have* seen this clock before! What was it about this clock that was so strange? Oh yes! Now you remember everything. You've read all about this weird cuckoo clock in a GOOSEBUMPS book—*The Cuckoo Clock of Doom.*

This looks like the very same clock that got that kid Michael Webster into so much trouble. His dad brought it home from an antique shop. He told Michael not to touch it. But Michael didn't listen. Curiosity got the better of him—and then so did the evil clock!

A terrible spell had been put on the clock. A strange spell. A dangerous spell that made Michael go backwards in time. It turned him into a little kid!

"Hmmmmmm," you wonder, "could this really be the very same clock?" You can't help wondering if that nasty little bird is still in there.

Turn to PAGE 71.

You wake up all right. But the minute you open your eyes you know something is very wrong. It's dark all round you. You have no idea where you are. Even if you could see, your head feels too heavy to turn and glance round.

"Kip? Abbey?" you call out.

Your own voice echoes back to you. You try to lift your hand and can't budge it. You try to move your leg. You can't. Your heart starts to race.

"Kip! Abbey!" you yell this time. But there's nothing. Only the feeling that you are trapped. Weighted down.

Your skin feels coated with something heavy and hard. Like iron . . . or like . . .

"*A suit of armour!*" you scream.

You hear the blood rushing in your ears. Or is it laughter?

Now you remember everything! You were feeling so sleepy. But just before you fell asleep, the Evil Knight's voice filled your head. "Be all the evil you can be. Join my army."

While you slept, the Evil Knight made you one of his Evil guards! You will have to serve his evil wishes for the rest of your little, evil life!

THE END

48

THUMP! You land on something soft. It's a body! A human body!

"Oomph! Please, get off me this instant!" A regal-looking boy dressed in tights and puffy shorts pushes you, Kip and Abbey off him. You all stand up and dust yourselves off.

"Who are you?" you ask the boy. He looks your age.

"I am a page," answers the boy. "Page forty-eight in a class of one hundred and forty-four."

"A page?" Abbey asks. "What's a page?"

"We are knights in training," the boy answers proudly.

"And *we're* trying to get *away* from a knight!" you remind Abbey.

"Can you show us the way out of here?" Kip asks.

Page forty-eight points to a gate that opens by itself. "That's the way out," he says. "It's the Valley of Rocks."

"Hurry!" you order Abbey and Kip. "The gate is closing!" You make it through just as the gate crashes down behind you. You look back. Page forty-eight has gone. All you see before you is a night sky and a strange, mysterious valley full of rocks.

Take the risky, rocky exit to PAGE 72.

"Okay, okay. The fun's over," you declare. You move over to the crate marked EVIL KNIGHT and start to loosen the straps holding it shut. It's still shaking a little, but the screaming has died down to a faint moan.

"You really had me going there for a minute," you continue. "Those screams sound pretty scary. And all that moaning and shaking? Wow, you two are good!"

Kip and Abbey look as if they don't know what you're talking about. But you know better.

"Who did you get to help you with this little prank, anyway? My dad?" you ask. Your dad is just the sort of joker to go in for something like this too.

You fumble with the leather straps, but you finally get them undone. By now you're chuckling to yourself. It really was a good prank. Complete with these oversized crates. Still, you can't believe you fell for it.

Speaking of falling, that's what the front door to the crate does next. It's also what your lower jaw does—it falls open. You try to scream but all that comes out is a little whimper.

There—in front of you—about thirty centimetres from your face—you stare into the laser-light eyes of the Knight in Screaming Armour!

Turn to PAGE 16, if you DARE!

50

You peer into the open crate. There's a flash of light. And then . . .

"There's nothing in this crate!" you exclaim. "I thought you said there was armour in here."

"There *was*," Abbey huffs, acting cool again. "But now it's gone, okay?"

"That's impossible!" Kip argues. "This crate weighed a tonne when we moved it in here!"

Abbey glances back at the empty crate. "Someone must have taken the armour, that's all. For crying out loud!" Oops, wrong thing to say: "*Eeeeeeeaaaa-hahahahaha!*" The bone-chilling scream of the Evil Knight turns to hideous, wicked laughter.

"It's the curse. The Evil Knight killed Sir Edmund Saxton, and now he's taken his armour!"

"What's next?" you say in disbelief. ". . . Or who?" Then you see something. There. Resting on the floor of the crate. A jagged piece of parchment paper. Do you pick it up? This curse thing is seeming less and less silly by the second.

If you pick the paper up and see what it says, turn to PAGE 70.

If you decide this whole business is too weird for your taste, and it's time to close the crate back up again and call the police, turn to PAGE 9.

So you think you're good at mazes, huh? Try to get yourself out of this one! Pick up a pencil and try to draw the escape route out of the maze below. Can you do it on your first try?

If you make it through, HOORAY FOR YOU! Face your next challenge on PAGE 75.

If you don't make it through, read your fate on PAGE 65.

The flashing eyes across the courtyard could only be one thing. The eyes of the Knight in Screaming Armour.

"We can't escape from him," Abbey sighs. "It's no use trying any more. He brought us here. This is his world."

"He must want something from us, otherwise he would have destroyed us by now," you point out.

"He's only toying with us," Abbey says bitterly. "Like a cat plays with its food."

"It's as if he's using our fear of him to make us face all other possible fears," Kip whispers mysteriously.

Abbey gives Kip a double take. "Face other fears? That's ridiculous!" she says. "I'm afraid of flying, but you don't see him making me fly."

A strong gust of wind blows through the bell tower and rings the bell. *BONG! BONG! BONG!* You clap your hands over your ears. Kip dives for the pile of monks' robes. Abbey jumps back and slams against the crumbling wall. The wall gives way behind her. "Help me! I'm fffff ... flying!"

Abbey soars higher and higher. Until she's out of sight.

"Abbey!" Kip cries. "Come back!"

If she doesn't come back, soar to PAGE 92.
If she returns in a flash, zoom to PAGE 102.

The bird turns right. "Where are you taking us?" you call to the black hawk.

"Aawwk! Aawwk!" squawks the giant, feathered bird.

"We shouldn't leave this place," Kip says worriedly. "If Abbey comes back she won't know where we went."

"And if we stay in the bell tower," you reason, "we won't be there when she gets back anyway. That beast looked pretty hungry."

As the flying speed increases, the flapping of the big bird's wings drowns out your voices. You fly in silence now. But you're just as worried about finding Abbey as Kip is. Your worry time is cut short when you look over the bird's shoulder and see a rocky side of a mountain straight ahead.

"Look out!" you scream as the bird heads right for it. "We're going to crash!"

The bird speeds up. The mountainside is directly in your flight path. "Stop!" you scream with all your might. "Can't you hear me? We're going to crash!"

Turn to PAGE 125.

54

You are dizzy from the heat and the force of the sword against your helmet. The Sorceress' shouts are echoed by the other evil creatures in the dungeon. "Fight! Fight!" they all cry at once.

"They want a fight? I'll give them a fight!" you say.

The Evil Knight raises his sword again and prepares to slash your suit in half. This is the hit that is aimed to destroy you.

You take one heavy step backwards. You raise your battleaxe high over the Evil Knight's black-armoured helmet. He swings his steel-bladed sword right at your stomach.

Think fast! With the heavy battleaxe raised over your head, you can't exactly duck! Instead, you pull your stomach back, as far as it will go. You turn yourself into a human question mark.

The mighty blow of the Evil Knight scratches across your armour with a ring. But it doesn't cut you.

You still have the axe raised over your head. You lower it now with all your strength. *CRASH!* In one swift motion you bring the axe down on the head of your evil enemy.

"AAAaaaaaaahhhh!" the Knight in Screaming Armour screams. But this time he falls to the dungeon floor.

He lies there motionless.

Quick! Find out if he's still alive on PAGE 111.

"SPLAT!"

"THWAAAAAT!"

"SOOOWAAACK!"

The Mud Slingers throw their mud faster than you can wipe it away.

Abbey gives up. She stands facing one muddy wall with her hands up over her mud-covered eyes. The monsters stand in front of her like a firing line. They scoop up new mud and pelt her.

You watch in horror as the flung mud covers every inch of her clothing, hair and skin. In no time Abbey is completely flattened into the mud-covered wall. In another second it is impossible to see where Abbey ends and the wall begins. She *is* the wall!

"Kip!" you shout. "Kip, where are you?"

While you were watching Abbey being *mud*-ified, Kip was being plastered to another wall. Only his eyes peer out at you. Then *"SCHWAAAAAP!"* he's gone.

You lunge towards the wall where Kip was. You scrape at the hardening mud. You try to say "Kip", but all that comes out of your mouth is a burbling mud burp.

"SWAAAAAAAAAT!" A warm mud-ball plasters your back. You fall face first into the wall of muck.

Hold your breath until you get to PAGE 17!

Then it hits you. You recognize that voice! "The cottage!" you exclaim. "It's the old man's voice from the cottage."

Now you can see him sitting in a rocking chair. He's hideous! He has THREE HEADS sprouting from his neck! And all six eyes are focused on *you*.

"Aawwk!" a black bird screeches from a cage above you. "Aawwk!"

The squawking bird looks familiar. There's hardwood beneath you now, so you step closer to examine the bird. It reaches up with its claw and flicks the feathers on the back of its head. An eerie feeling comes over you.

"It's Abbey!" Kip shrieks. "Abbey's turned into a bird!"

The black bird screeches back at you.

"Birds of a feather flock together," the old man cackles as he wiggles one bony finger in your direction.

That's all it takes. Feathers burst through every pore of your skin. Your nose and mouth fuse together and harden. You scream, but all that comes out is an "Aaawwwk!"

"Aaaawwwk!" the three of you squawk.

"That's it, my fine-feathered friends," croaks the old man. "Sing for me, my pretties! Sing!"

"Aaaawwk!" you all sing, which, when translated, means

THE END.

THAT WHAT IS NOW IS NOT WHAT'S REAL! you repeat in your head. *Louder! Harder! Concentrate! THAT WHAT IS NOW IS NOT WHAT'S REAL!*

Then . . . a miracle happens.

The shrinking room starts getting bigger again. Slowly it returns to normal size. The lightning bolt outlines round each cousin fade to a dim glow and then disappear!

"Just like the Mud Slingers," you declare. "Another trick of our imaginations! This Evil Knight likes to play mind games, I'm afraid."

"*You're* afraid!" Abbey sputters. She tries to smooth down her fly-away hair. "I'm terrified! I may never get my hair to curl after this!"

As if in response to Abbey's complaint, the only remaining door swings open. By itself. Out comes a voice that makes the blood curdle in your veins. It's the voice of the Evil Knight. And he's whispering your name . . .

You must answer. Go to PAGE 31.

58

You don't always agree with Abbey, but this time you decide to take her advice. "You're right," you say. "Only a fool would go in there!"

Before you can say another word, you feel yourself being pulled against your will. "COME FORWARD, FOOL!" the Evil Knight commands.

"Who-o-o-o? M-m-m-me?" you stammer.

Yes, you! Turn to PAGE 128.

Kip decides the right door is the left one. He reaches for the handle on the left. When his hand is only centimetres from it, sparks fly off the handle. Kip jumps back. "Whoa! It's electrically charged!" he cries.

You stop holding the walls apart long enough to reach for the door handle. More sparks shoot into the air. A rapid-fire zapping noise crackles around you. It sounds like the insect zapper on the roof of the Dairy Queen on a muggy summer night.

You try the door one more time. *ZZZZAPPPPPPP!* A charge of electrical current sputters and sparks first around Abbey, then around you, and finally around Kip.

The three of you light up like electrical garden ornaments at Christmastime. Abbey's long blonde hair stands straight up. Sparks fly from each individual strand. She's a human firework, and so are you and Kip!

You try to turn back and escape the shock treatment, but you have no choices here.

Go to PAGE 24.

Abbey rushes towards the wall of doors. She's just about to reach the handle on the first door when her foot slips on something. "Another piece of parchment!" she cries out.

You and Kip run to join her. She holds a jagged-edged scrap of parchment in her hands. It's just like the other one you found. She reads it to you:

"... *beware his deadly charge and feel* ...

That's it. That's all it says."

"There's got to be more," you insist.

"Deadly charge," Abbey repeats. "I know about charging things. Sounds like someone's going to be doing some killer shopping!"

"Very funny," Kip says sarcastically.

"Maybe not to a jerk like you," Abbey shoots back.

"Oh yeah?" Kip threatens.

"Good comeback," Abbey taunts.

"Hey, hold it. Hold it," you say. "We need to work together here. These scraps of paper are obviously meant to be clues. I've got a feeling they'll lead us to the missing armour, if we pay attention. Until then anything could happen."

Go to PAGE 62.

Kip turns and sees the beast creeping up the stairs. "Stay still and maybe it won't see us," you whisper.

Slowly, you and Kip press yourselves into a corner of the bell tower and watch the beast. You've never seen anything like it.

It's as large as the biggest lion and as black as night. It has short ears set back on a small doglike head. A long, swishing tail hits the crumbling wall, knocking stones to the ground.

The beast growls. Rows of shiny white teeth drip with saliva. It turns its fierce eyes in your direction. It sniffs the air. It smells you! A long red tongue licks its drooling black lips. It sees you!

"It's going to pounce!" you cry.

The beast jumps for you, but you jump too. Right over the wall of the bell tower with Kip right behind you.

"Oh, nooooooooo!" you both scream on your way down.

"Aawwk! Aawwk!" you hear. A giant nighthawk passes you as you fall. "Aawwk!" the bird squawks again as it swoops down beneath your falling bodies.

Fall down to PAGE 95.

You take the other scrap of parchment out of your pocket and try to fit the two pieces together. None of the edges match up.

"Never mind that stupid puzzle!" Abbey bursts out. "I want to get out of here *now!*"

Without waiting another second, Abbey runs to the other side of the room and tries the knob on the first door. But as she turns it, the door disappears and becomes solid white wall again!

She tries the next door. Gone!

And the next one. And the next one. And the next one.

Gone. Gone. Gone. Right from under her hand!

"If the doors keep disappearing, we'll be stuck in here for ever!" Kip says in a panic.

"We have to get out," you shout. "And fast! Look! These walls are closing in on us! We'll be crushed!"

Inch by inch the floor space narrows. The walls are grinding in on your little group.

"Try another door, Abbey!" Kip screams, as the wall behind him pushes against his back. "The room is shrinking! We'll be squashed like bugs!"

Evil laughter booms through the shrinking room. "He's here!" Abbey shrieks. "The Knight in Screaming Armour. He's here!"

Squeeze through to PAGE 89.

Your hunch is right! When you hold the muddy glop up to the light, it disappears! You grab another Mud Slinger, hold it up, look right through it, and it too disappears!

Now Kip and Abbey are snagging Mudmen too. One by one the grubby gremlins are grabbed and held up to the light. Soon the whole muddy mass of them disappears and the walls turn white.

You and your cousins fall in a heap on the floor. "Whew!" Kip tries to catch his breath. "Was that close, or what?"

"And really disgusting!" Abbey adds. "I appreciate a good mud facial as much as the next girl, but that was ridiculous."

"It was a pretty dirty trick." You actually agree with Queen Abbey for a change. "But now what? We still haven't found that missing armour. Do we just walk on out of here and go home?"

"You said it, cousin!" Abbey's not too worried about any missing suits of armour.

"I don't know," Kip says. "Dad is going to go berserk when he finds out we've lost the Sir Edmund suit! He'll be here next week. If we don't find it, I don't want to be the one to open the door for him!"

"Speaking of doors," Abbey interrupts, "look over there! There's a whole wall of doors. One of them has to be the way out of this stuffy room."

Turn to PAGE 60.

Everything's ready. The fight of the ages is about to begin. Wearing the armour of the Good Knight should give you courage. Instead it's giving you a rash. You start to itch like crazy. I must have an allergy to silver polish, you think to yourself.

You hear the wretched voice of the Sorceress echoing inside your armoured suit. Is she casting some kind of wicked itching spell on you?

"When spells come from a Sorceress' kitchen
The silver knight shall start to itchin'!
A suit of armour will not stay
The rash that never goes away!"

You rip your steel gloves off as fast as you can. You fumble at the hinge to your breastplate and manage to swing it open. You start to scratch but it doesn't seem to help. You're itching all over now. Just then you hear a horrible scream. "AAAAaaahhh!"

"Uh-oh," you say to yourself. "Here comes trouble!" The Evil Knight is here to fight. But all you can do is scratch! You might be itching for a fight, but it looks like this fight's been scratched!

THE END

You and your cousins are desperate. You've tried for days to find your way out of the maze of hedges. No luck.

You're weak. Tired. And, most of all, hungry. That's when you kind of lose it.

You never make it out of the hedges alive.

And years later, your bodies are absorbed into the fertile soil. The roots of the hedges find you very tasty.

Basically, you're PLANT FOOD!

THE END

"Aaaaaaaahhhhhhh!" You don't know who's screaming louder, you or the Evil Knight. You stare into his glowing eyes! You feel the steam of his breath on your face! And then he reaches out, lifts you up, and flings you over the mountainside.

Down, down, down you tumble.

Your arms and legs bash against the sharp rocks. You can feel the bumps and bruises starting to swell even before you reach the rocky bottom of the mountain.

At last you tumble to a stop next to the motionless figures of Kip and Abbey. You don't move a muscle—because you can't. You're stiff all over and you're getting stiffer. And stiffer . . . And stiffer . . .

THE END

"Yeah. It's the *middle* of the night to be exact," the shadow answers.

You recognize her voice. "Abbey!" you gasp. "What are you doing in my room?"

"I heard you screaming," she says, holding her hands over her ears. "Horrible, horrible screams. What's going on here? I'm trying to get some sleep!"

"Evil," Kip whispers as he peeks through the doorway behind Abbey. "That's what's going on here." In the dim rays of the hall night-light you see panic on Kip's face.

"Don't be ridiculous!" Abbey scolds her brother. "The only evil going on here is that I'm losing my beauty sleep! This screaming simply has to stop! Now shut your mouth and go back to bed!"

"It won't stop," Kip insists. "It's the curse. I know it. We shouldn't have brought that rusty old armour. Now we've woken the spirit of the Evil Knight. There's no escaping it. Not for the Saxtons!"

You don't know about this whole curse thing. But one thing you do know. There's no way you can go back to sleep and pretend you can't hear the screams. The Knight in Screaming Armour *cannot* and *will not* be ignored.

Turn to PAGE 19.

68

The middle clock face has no hands so you can't reset the time. You study this orange clock face for a moment and decide not to play with it now. Instead you slip the whole clock under your sweatshirt. "This might come in handy later," you say to Kip and Abbey. "You never know when we might need more time."

As soon as you say the word "time" every clock in this clock-filled room strikes the hour: *BONG! BONG! CUCKOO! TICKTOCK BONG! TOCK TICKTOCK CUCKOO! CUCKOO! BONG! BONG! BONG!!!!*

The noise is almost unbearable. You try to cover your ears, but you only have one hand free. It's as if the clocks are striking back! It's as if they're angry at you for taking one of them! You tighten your grip on the three-faced clock and head for the exit door. "Let's get out of here!" you shout to the others. "Hurry!"

Turn to PAGE 7.

"Wheeeeeeee!" Abbey yells. Her hair flies out behind her as you zoom faster and faster down the spiralling slide.

The force of the wind in Kip's face pulls his cheeks back in a permanent smile. Faster and faster you go. Around and around. "Wheeeee!" changes to "Whoa!" You're starting to feel sick. You wonder if this ride will *ever end*!

You try to keep your chin against your chest so the wind doesn't throw your head back. You try to swallow so you won't throw up. It's almost more than you can take! Then you notice that the spirals are getting tighter. Two more vicious spins and then *WHAM!* You slam to a stop.

Your head is spinning. Your ears are ringing. Your nose is pressed up against a wall of glass.

"Where are we now?" Kip manages to say. You're not sure you want to know the answer. But above you, you can see two buttons. One says HEADS. The other says TALES.

"I think we've got to choose," you announce.

"I'm not choosing," Kip declares.

"Leave me alone," is all Abbey can say.

You reach into your pocket and pull out a coin.

Toss a coin to help you decide which button to push. If you push HEADS, turn to PAGE 103.
If you push TALES, turn to PAGE 26.

You bend down and pick up the jagged-edged piece of parchment. There's writing on it. "Hey, look what I've found!" you exclaim. "It's a note. Or a piece of one." You read it:

> *"Only a knight, and Saxton born*
> *Can break the curse that now we mourn.*
> *But they who wear Sir Edmund's steel*
> *Must prove their courage and strength are real.*
> *Before the break of day brights light*
> *One Good shall fight one Evil Knight . . .*

That's funny. It sounds like a challenge."

"How boring," Abbey complains.

"They who wear Sir Edmund's steel," you read again. "What do you think that means?"

"The armour," Kip replies. "Sir Edmund's armour."

"But it's gone," you point out.

"That scrap of paper looks like it's been torn from something," Kip adds. "If we could find more pieces of the poem, maybe we can figure out where the missing armour is. It's like a puzzle."

"That's the stupidest thing I've ever heard," Abbey says. Then she rubs her eyes. "I'm sleepy."

Kip yawns a big yawn. You feel it, too. An overwhelming urge to fall asleep. You let yourself curl up on the floor and . . .

If you wake up and are with your cousins, turn to PAGE 20.

If you wake up all alone, turn to PAGE 47.

You've just got to know if this is the same clock as the one in the GOOSEBUMPS book. It was such an amazing story. You reach up to the little door just over the clock face. It slides open. You peer inside.

"*CUCKOOOO!*" Out flies the most hideous bird you've ever seen. Is it the cuckoo bird of doom? You fall to the ground. You've got to protect your face from that bird! You wrap your hands so tightly across your face that you block out all the air. There's a fluttering and a scraping on your skin. Seconds later, you black out.

When you wake up, you don't remember anything. You feel quite strange but you don't exactly feel younger like Michael Webster was. Smaller, yes. But not younger. What's happened to you?

A steady *tick*, *tock*, *tick* booms through the darkness around you—slowly, slowly. Then a little door slides open in front of you. You rush through it and squawk, "*Cuckoo! Cuckoo! Cuckoo!*" You ruffle your feathers! "I'm a bird!" you screech.

But then it's over. That's it. Until the next hour.

Guess it wasn't the cuckoo clock of doom after all. More like the cuckoo clock of craziness. You're still alive, but all this noise and waiting is going to drive you cuckoo in

THE END.

You've landed in a valley. But the green hills of a moment ago have long gone. In fact, there isn't a blade of grass as far as the eye can see. It's all rocks. Broken up shards and boulders and stones. And it's dark. A pale moon shines up above.

Abbey tries to move and barely balances on a wobbly platform of stone. She shrieks, "This is like an avalanche waiting to happen!"

"Be careful!" Kip warns. "These flat rocks aren't as steady as they look."

"Yeah, uh, thanks for the tip, Kip," Abbey says. "I think we noticed!"

They're right. The rock you're standing on tips and throws you backwards to another flat rock below. "Whoa!" you cry as your new rocky floor see-saws up and down. You glance down. There are more jagged rocks waiting to catch you below.

Next you look up. And something flashes. High up on the rocky point of this mountain, something silvery shimmers in the moonlight. It seems to be calling to you. What is it?

Climb over to PAGE 28.

You let go of the rope and rush over to the kettle. If you can only lift it, you could throw the liquid on the ghosts. That should scatter them.

The hooded robed figures make their way up the steps. They're getting closer! You're getting frantic. You strain against the handle of the kettle with all your strength. It budges a little and some of the liquid sloshes on to the stone floor. It pools around your foot. And you SLIP!

You fall back, arms flailing. You knock against the bell. *BONG! BONG! BONG! BONG!* the bell tolls.

The monks' chant changes: *"The bell tolls for us! The bell tolls for us! The bell tolls for us!"* One by one the hooded figures slump to the floor of the bell tower. Soon they are nothing more than a pile of empty robes in a heap at your feet.

BONG! BONG! BONG! You push the bell again. Kip and Abbey pull off their hoods. "You saved us!" Kip cries gratefully.

"And those stupid ghosts have gone for good!" Abbey adds. "Can you believe those monks? Get a life. I mean, get a death."

You breathe a sigh of relief. "We're safe now," you say. All is still—all except the flashing eyes on the other side of the courtyard.

"Uh-oh," you say. "Those eyes can only mean one thing."

Turn to PAGE 52 . . . if you dare.

74

What began as a rescue mission is now a mission to destroy you. The giant black nighthawk zooms upwards.

"Hang on!" you shout to Kip. He clings to one slick black feather sticking out from the bird's back.

The hawk swoops down suddenly. It's trying to shake you off! You fly out to the side of the wings and your body flaps freely in the wind. "Whoooaaaa!" you yell.

This roller-coaster bird ride is making your stomach do flip-flops. Kip looks just as airsick as you feel. But it's not over yet. Now the hawk does loop-the-loops until at last you can't hold on any longer.

You let go. "Goodbye, Kip!" you call out as you start free-falling! "Goodby-y-y-y-y-y-y-e-e-e-e-e-e-e."

Turn to PAGE 117.

The hedges are behind you. The green hills are in front of you. There's a warm wind in your face and something . . . something is coming over those hills. A dark, black mist is rolling towards you. It's already halfway to where you're standing.

"I don't like the look of this," Kip says.

The warm wind picks up. Dark clouds gather. Dust whips around in whirlpools. Evil is in the air around you.

"Look," you remark, "sooner or later we're going to have to face this Evil Knight. That's the only way to break the curse, right? Only a Saxton can defeat him!"

"I'd prefer later to sooner—" Kip starts to answer back. He never finishes his sentence.

"*SCREEEEEEEEEEEEEEEEEEEEEEEEEE-EEEEEEEE!*" The scream of the Evil Knight announces his arrival.

Find out what happens next on PAGE 85!

You read the words of the new puzzle piece again: "That what is NOW is not what's real." You don't know what this means yet, but you do know you have to get out of this room NOW!

"Zzzzt?" Kip sparks.

"Zzzt zzzztttz zzt?" Abbey adds.

They think you have figured something out. They want to know what is happening NOW. You cannot answer NOW, because you understand what this puzzle piece means. There never is a NOW. As soon as NOW comes, it becomes THEN. In the split second that is NOW you know one thing, there is no escaping this place NOW. There is no NOW. Just as you are about to escape NOW, NOW is THEN and your chances of leaving have gone.

You and Kip and Abbey are stuck in the neverland of NOW. The awful truth is closing in on you and so are the walls. What is NOW is not what's real. But what *is* real is that for you and Kip and Abbey, NOW is

THE END.

The voice is soft. "Come in," it says again. You stand up, feeling dizzy from floating. You fall forward through the door. *You're in*. The door closes softly behind you. You breathe a sigh of relief until a steel barred gate CRASHES down over the door!

"AAAAAAaaaaaaaaahhhhhhhh!" the scream of the Evil Knight rings out. "WELCOME TO MY KNIGHT-MARE!" he bellows.

You turn your head left, then right. "This isn't a cottage!" you cry. "It's a dungeon!"

Giant black rats scurry over your feet. Long-haired poisonous spiders scamper across their webs to hang down in your face. Heads without bodies float through the air. Clocks without hands scream out "Cuckoo cuckoo!" A Mud Slinging monster throws a glob of gooey stuff at you. You duck just in time. *THWACK!* It splatters against a stone wall.

Lightning bolts zap and *zzzzttt* in the air above you. Vampire bats fly blindly through the iron bars of the gate behind you. No, this is not a cottage. This is a Den of Danger! A Hall of Horrors! An Alcove of Evil! The Final Frontier!

Turn to PAGE 130.

You stare at the walls of greenery surrounding you. "The hedges are too high," you say. "We can't climb over them."

"It looks like a maze," Abbey comments. "You know, Kip, like they used to have at royal palaces and places like that? I wonder if there's a way out."

"We'll either have to find our way out or break through the hedge. We can't stay in here for ever," you say.

"For ever!" Kip wails.

"Knock it off, Kip!" you and Abbey both cry.

So what will it be?

If you try to find your way out, turn to PAGE 51.

If you try to break through the hedge instead, turn to PAGE 116.

Where the queen's head was, Abbey's head now rests. On Abbey's neck the queen's head straightens itself and stares right at you! The new Queen Abbey stands peering at the glass door trying to catch her own reflection.

Kip hasn't noticed what's happened to Abbey yet. He's busy making faces at a hideous gargoyle head along the wall. The grotesque, bald, wide-mouthed, bulging-eyed head is the ugliest head in the room.

"A face only a mother could love," Kip jokes, gazing into the monster's beady little eyes. In a flash, the gargoyle head changes places with Kip's!

You watch in stunned amazement as Kip, the Gargoyle, turns on Abbey, the Queen. "Argh!" says Kip.

"Aahhh!" the startled Queen Abbey screams. "Guards! Off with his head! Off with his head!"

A whole row of Royal Guard heads springs to life. The helmeted sentries cry out from their stands, "Save the Queen! Save the Queen!" With one quick motion the whole row of guards' heads tips forward and rolls on to the floor. They regroup into formation and start rolling full force towards Kip! In seconds he'll be buried in heads!

If you use your head to help Kip, turn to PAGE 30.

If you use someone else's head to help Kip, turn to PAGE 11.

80

The Good Knight's armour has armed you with more than a battleaxe and shield. It's armed you with courage. This dungeon doesn't scare you. "Show your face, Evil Knight!" you shout bravely. You don't have to wait long.

A giant figure steps out of the sickly yellow light. It is the Evil Knight! He is taller, darker and more scary than ever. His eyes shoot flames at you. The flames hit your silver armour and heat it up on contact. His eyes fire at you again! Sweat pours down your face and neck. Inside the armour barbecue pit you're melting!

The Evil Knight laughs as he raises his sword and swings it hard against your helmet. The vibrations from the metal-on-metal make your whole body shake. The Evil Knight swings again and hits you on the other side of your helmet. You're too stunned to move.

"Fight!" someone screams. It's the Sorceress. The same one who created the Evil Knight and watched him defeat Sir Edmund Saxton. She's been waiting centuries for another showdown. "Fight!" she screams again. "Fight! Fight! Fight!"

Take a deep breath and go to PAGE 54.

"Look at this one!" Abbey calls out. She's pointing to an antique cuckoo clock standing on the floor in a corner.

The clock is mostly black. But its designs are painted with silver, gold and blue, and it's decorated with scrolls, carvings, knobs and buttons. It has a white face and gold hands and numbers.

You glance at the clock and feel an odd sense of doom about it. You wouldn't be at all surprised if the door opened up and a hideous bird flew out! Something about this clock looks strangely familiar to you. Where have you seen it before?

If you think you know where you've seen this clock before, turn to PAGE 46.

If another clock hanging on the wall next to this one catches your eye, turn to PAGE 93.

82

You run to where the cottage is, but it's no longer there! Those nasty pixies keep moving it.

"Over here!" the pixies giggle.

"Over there!"

"Over here!"

"Over there!"

"Over here!"

"Over there!"

Run until you drop on PAGE 104.

"Abbey!" Kip cries as he watches his sister twist in the grasp of the Evil Knight.

"Help me!" Abbey cries in terror.

CRASH! The Evil Knight's other armoured arm rips through the wooden slats of the crate and wraps around Abbey's body. You and Kip scream in a harmony of horror. Any hopes you had of helping Abbey vanish as the Knight continues crashing through his wooden prison. Nothing can stop him now!

He's going to destroy all that is good—and that means YOU!

Cover your eyes. Don't look. This is going to be too terrible to watch. Evil spelled backwards is LIVE, which is one thing you won't do when the Knight in Screaming Armour has finished with you!

THE END

Or is it the end really? If you think it's too early to exit this adventure, go to PAGE 99.

You decide you need all the help you can get. Kip and Abbey are just on the other side of that door, you think.

You turn back towards the door. As if in answer to your thoughts, a huge iron grating slams into the ground in front of you. Another sheet of metal slams down in front of the grating.

"Kip! Abbey!" you call to them. Then all the monsters from your nightmares start rattling their cages.

"You'll never win!" the warty women sing out together. "You cannot win without the Good Knight's armour. Evil is as Evil does and Evil does do evil!" They cackle in their cages, taunting you with their wicked words.

You force yourself not to listen to them. You know what you have to do now. You have to stand firmly and fight the Evil Knight on your own.

"Show your face, Evil Knight!" you call out.

The dragon spews a stream of fire, lighting the darkest corners of the Hall of Evil. Still you see no Evil Knight.

"Show your face, Evil Knight!" you shout again.

Don't lose your courage now. Turn to PAGE 118.

The Evil Knight's screams mingle with the whistling blast of hot wind. You can almost feel his evil breath mixed in with the wind. You know he's so close. The dark mist rushes at you!

The force of the gale throws the three of you backwards against the hedge. But you don't feel the prickly leaves. You don't land on the ground where you were before. In fact, you don't land at all!

"We're faaaaaaaaaaaaaaalling!" the three of you cry together. Falling!

Falling!

Falling!

If the chair you're sitting on has a cushion, turn to PAGE 48.

If it doesn't have a cushion, or you're not sitting on a chair, turn to PAGE 72.

There's no way you're going to just stand here and be mudified by a tribe of mud-slinging mud monsters!

"Come on!" you shout. You duck a far-flung mud pie aimed right for your face. "We're getting out of here!"

"Which way is out?" Abbey cries. She throws her hands up and blocks a blob of ooze. As she blocks the blob, you notice the light from the bare bulb swinging right through the Mud Slinger!

Suddenly an idea clicks in your mind. "I've got a hunch this is just one big dirty trick being played on us by the Evil Knight," you guess. "These Mud Slingers aren't real. They've been planted in our minds by the powers of the Knight. The light shines right through them. Watch!"

You reach for the biggest, muddiest mass of glop and grab it by the neck. Your hands sink down into his shoulders. Still you manage to lift the barrel-bodied beast up over your head.

If you hold the mud beast up to the light, turn to PAGE 63.

If you throw it down to the ground, turn to PAGE 29.

You can't help it. The SLAM of the door makes you scream.

"We didn't mean to scare you." It's the old man's voice.

"We?" you ask. "Did you say *we*?"

To answer your question, the old man hobbles forward. You see his dusty boots emerge from the shadows. A pair of ragged canvas trousers and a cardigan sweater with holes appear. Then you see his face.

Talk about U-G-L-Y! He cackles as he glares at you from a wrinkled, mole-covered face. This man must be a hundred years old. And he's looking at you strangely.

Then something catches your eye. Something next to his grizzled old ear. IT'S ANOTHER HEAD! A horrible, wart-covered, puffy-eyed head with a squirming, dangling tongue! It's sticking out from the right side of his neck!

You hear Abbey squealing in terror.

And there's ANOTHER HEAD! On the other side! Sticking out from his neck. As this one catches the light you see a mouthful of slimy rotting teeth. His bloodshot eyes roll around out of control!

"We didn't mean to scare you," the old man says. "WE MEANT TO TERRIFY YOU!"

If you can, run to PAGE 98.
If you're frozen in terror, turn to PAGE 108.

"*No bell tolls for us. No bell tolls for us. No bell tolls for us.*" Kip's and Abbey's voices rise above the others.

You gaze into their transparent eyes and catch a glimpse of your own reflection.

Under the hood of your robe there's NO FACE AT ALL!

"*No bell tolls for us! No bell tolls for us!*" you hear yourself say. "*No bell tolls for us.*"

Face it—you're a dead ringer until

THE END.

You can't see the Evil Knight, but you know he's here somewhere. His hideous laughter turns to screams and back to laughter again. This shrinking room is a tiny torture chamber. And it's getting tinier by the second.

You brace yourself against one of the advancing walls in a frantic attempt to hold it back. You strain against it with all of your strength. "Aaaaaaaaaaaah!" you yell as your muscles begin to burn and ache. "Try another door, Abbey!" you gasp out. "Quick!" But Abbey is paralysed with fear. She doesn't move a muscle.

Your ear is pushed up against the crushing wall. There is a terrible grinding sound behind it. Your feet start to skid and slip.

"The door, Kip! The door!" you scream.

"But there are two doors left," Kip cries. "Which door should I open?"

"The right one!" you yell back. "Open the right one!"

If the door on the right is the right one, turn to PAGE 42.

If the door on the left is the right one, turn to PAGE 59.

"WELCOME TO *MY* MUSEUM!" roars the voice of the Evil Knight as you enter the mysterious dark room. "MY VERY OWN MID-*EVIL* MUSEUM OF EVIL KNIGHT-MARES!" He bursts into laughter at his own joke. His horrifying laughter mocks you. It seems to come from every direction.

You spin round, peering into the darkness for any sign of the Knight. "Where are you?" you shout over the chorus of evil sounds. "Show your face!"

"AAAAAAAAAAAAHHHHHHHHHHHH!" An ear-piercing screech. The Knight in Screaming Armour reminds you who's in charge here. Suddenly you don't feel so curious any more.

A dim light seems to come from somewhere. Or maybe it's just that your eyes grow accustomed to the dark. But all around you vertical lines seem to emerge from the blackness. They're bars. Iron bars. They're CAGES! But they're not *your* cage. At least, not yet.

It's a kind of museum exhibit. Or maybe a zoo. A zoo of evil. You shake with terror when you see what's inside all those cages.

See what's in the cages on PAGE 106.

"*Zzzzt! Zzzzt! Zzzt zzzt zzttt!*" You try to speak, but the only things coming out of your mouth are sparks!

"*Zzzzt zzzt!*" Abbey adds her two sparks.

"*Zzzzzzzzt! Zzzzzzzt!*" Kip sparks loudest of all. He's holding up the second piece of parchment with the warning about "his deadly charge".

If you could talk you would remind Kip—you've already seen that piece of the puzzle. You suppose that this electrically charged state you're all in is what the piece of parchment warned about.

Kip waves the parchment at you. "*Zzzzt zt!*" he says.

"*Zzt zzzzt!*" you agree. Sure you'll take another look at the piece of parchment. You try to see through all the sparks to what is written there. Here's the real shocker—new words have appeared! You read to yourself:

> *. . . beware his deadly charge and feel*
> *That what is NOW is not what's real.*

Aha! Now you get it!

If what you get is what you see, turn to PAGE 34.

If what you get is what you wish you'd never seen, turn to PAGE 76.

"Kip! Kip!" Abbey's voice is so far away now, you can hardly hear her.

"Wow! She's really flying!" you say in amazement. "You must be right about the fear thing, Kip."

"Come back!" Kip calls up to the night sky.

But Abbey's growing smaller and smaller against the night sky. And in another moment, she's gone. You almost can't believe it. Just like that. Gone.

Kip starts to sob.

You try to be brave. "We'll find her again. I know we will," you say. "We've come this far together. Through all this craziness."

A low growl from the stone stairs lets you know there's more craziness to come. "Who's there?" you demand.

"Aaaaaahhhhhhhhhhhh!" The Evil Knight's scream echoes out across the courtyard.

The growl on the stairs turns to a howl answering the scream of the Knight! Then, a huge, black catlike creature with yellow eyes appears around the bend in the stairs.

"Kip. Over there," you say as quietly as you can.

Turn to PAGE 61.

The antique cuckoo clock in the corner is strange. But it's nothing compared to the clock hanging on the wall next to it! "This clock looks like something from the future," you say to Kip and Abbey.

"It's pretty. Like me," Abbey declares. "I'm taking it down to get a closer look." She stands on tiptoe and lifts the square clock down. You all gather around to see. The shimmering, silver hologram clock face has three smaller clock faces on it. One face is silvery-green with wavy silver hands. One is hot pink with straight black hands. The one in the middle is fiery orange with no hands at all.

"They're set at different times," you notice. You check your watch. It's 1:00 a.m. You decide to reset the funny clock faces to the correct time.

To turn the hands on the green clock face first, go to PAGE 5.

To turn the hands on the pink clock face first, go to PAGE 109.

If you're fascinated by the orange clock face instead, turn to PAGE 68.

There are hedgehogs squirming all over you. They jabber away: "*Chitter . . . chee chee chitter chirt . . . chim chitter cheech.*"

"They're talking to each other!" you mutter through a mouthful of hedgehog spines. Two hedgehogs are holding a meeting right on your face. It doesn't feel very good. You manage to sit up. Dozens of the balled-up hedgehogs roll off you then pounce on you again.

"*Chirt cheett churnchit cheeeet!*" the lead hedgehog squeals. Three hedgehogs nesting in Abbey's hair look up.

The ones on Kip's shoulders curl into balls and roll down his chest. Spiny fur balls roll out of your sleeves, off your head, out of Abbey's hair, and even out from inside your shoes!

"*Chirt cheett churnchit cheeeet!*" the biggest hedgehog says again. In a flash, they scurry back into the hedges behind you.

What's going on? You feel a blast of wind. It's warm, not cold. You raise your eyes up to the hills. A dark mist is rolling down over them.

"Hey," you say. "We'd better get out of here. Whatever that mist is, those little animals were scared of it."

"Where are we going to go?" Abbey asks.

If you return to the hedges, turn to PAGE 23.
If you wait where you are to see what's coming, turn to PAGE 75.

You're falling fast, but not fast enough to escape hot drool dripping from the beast's mouth. The beast leans over the edge of the bell tower wall. You get a faceful of steaming spit. Before the next big gob hits you, the giant nighthawk flies under you and Kip. It catches you on its back and swoops upwards.

You don't know where this black bird of night is taking you. As you look back at the beast you know one thing for sure: wherever you're going has got to be better than where you've just been!

If the bird turns left, turn to PAGE 115.
If the bird turns right, turn to PAGE 53.
If the rescue mission takes a turn for the worse, turn to PAGE 74.

"You can just forget that Screaming Armour story!" Abbey snaps before Kip gets a chance to answer you. "It's really stupid and it's not even true."

But long after everyone has gone to sleep, you lie awake thinking about the crates in your garage.

Hours later, you've just dozed off when you are awakened by a chilling scream—and it's coming from the garage.

"The curse!" you gasp.

If you try to ignore the scream, turn to PAGE 13.

If you investigate the chilling shriek, turn to PAGE 19.

Led by the Evil Knight, the whole herd of sheep stampedes! Terror grips you, as the thundering herd bears down on the three of you. You are about to be trampled!

The stampede sounds like a sonic boom. You wrap your arms round your head and wait to feel the pain of a hundred little hooves pounding you into the grass. So this is how he plans to destroy us, you think. You open your mouth to scream, but you can't hear anything over the thundering of sheep feet.

Then, suddenly, there's nothing but the sound of screaming. Your own screaming. You peek through your arms.

The stampeding herd has gone. The hills have gone. All that's left are thorn bushes. You're buried in thorn bushes. And they hurt!

Turn to PAGE 132.

Leaving the three-faced monster behind, the three of you lunge for the back door of the cottage. "Locked again!" you cry, shaking the handle furiously.

"The key!" Kip reminds you. "Try the key!"

You fumble in your pocket, pull out the key and put it in the lock. Just as you feel the key start to turn, you hear the monster trio chanting a series of mumbo-jumbo words:

"Sliziwick, whizaslick, haggedly zee.
Make three into one with the turn of the key!"

The key turns. The door opens. The three of you push against each other trying to be the first one out.

You push. Kip pushes harder. Abbey pushes hardest! She pushes too hard.

The monster's spell has worked. All that pushing squashes your bodies together into one.

POP! You fall outside.

But the turn of the key has made you a three-faced, one-bodied monster just like the old man! All you know is two heads may be better than one, but three heads add up to one big headache!

THE END

"The end?" you challenge. "In your dreams, you hunk of junk! You won't get rid of us so fast."

Much to your cousins' surprise, you spring into action. You reach past the Knight to a shelf on the garage wall. You grab a can of motor oil and flip open the pop-top. You pour it over the armoured arms that hold Abbey in a deadly grip.

"Aahh!" Abbey shrieks as the oily liquid covers her head. But thanks to the oil, she slides right through the circling arms of iron. She's free!

Now you can get back to the business of closing up the EVIL KNIGHT crate. The three of you grab hammers, nails and ropes from the garage workbench. The Evil Knight's arms flail about. They're covered in the thick goopy oil. You hurry to seal up the wooden crate again.

It feels great to be back in control of things again. But the feeling doesn't last. Now the crate marked GOOD KNIGHT is rattling. A white light pierces right through the wood slats and zooms in on you, almost blinding you. The door pops open, ripping the leather straps. A vision of a knight, a knight in shining armour, fills your view. You squint and shield your eyes with your hands. The face on the knight is YOUR face!

The bright light fades away. You're left staring into the crate at a floating piece of parchment.

Pick it up on PAGE 70.

100

"Let's go to the right," Kip says as he pulls prickles from his arms and legs. "I don't like the look of that cottage over there. Why would anyone live out here in the middle of nowhere?"

A pixie giggles and the cottage disappears! "Now it's over here, not over there!" The pixie laughs. "Do you like it over here?" The cottage magically appears behind you. "Or do you like it over here?" Another pixie giggles as the cottage turns up on your left.

"Over here. Over there. It doesn't really matter where," the two pixies sing together. "Where you are is where you're not, when a pixie's spell you've got!"

"You should take the chance to hide," one sings, pointing to the magic cottage. "The Wicked One won't look inside," the other one sings.

The sudden shrill shriek of the Evil Knight sets your feet running. "If the Evil Knight destroys us before we can break the curse, no Saxton will ever be safe," you pant as you run. "He's coming. Hurry! We have to go and hide in that cottage over there. Like it or not!"

Run to the cottage on PAGE 82.

You lie there among the rocks for a moment. Your head is still spinning from your fall.

"Are you all right?" Abbey asks.

"We saw the whole thing!" Kip says with admiration. "I give it a perfect ten. You were fantastic!"

"I thought *you* were turning to stone!" you sputter.

"Ha! That's a good one." Abbey laughs. "We were just trying to keep still. We didn't want to start an avalanche while you were up there."

"Yeah," Kip explains. "It's just like with snow. The slightest movement or sound might bring everything tumbling down."

That's it. An avalanche. "Kip, you're a genius!" you exclaim.

"I am?"

"He is?" Abbey looks amazed.

"An avalanche. That's the way to get that shimmering thing. It will help us. I just know it. And if not, maybe an avalanche can help us to get out of this horrible place," you explain.

Before they can stop you, you pick up a good-sized rock and throw it as far as you can up the slope.

Pieces of rock start to cascade down the rock face. You, Kip and Abbey scramble to the edge of the slope out of the way.

Scramble over to PAGE 121.

In a flash, Abbey is back. But she's not Abbey any more. At least not most of her. It's her head—complete with long blonde hair—on the body of a gigantic black bird. Nighthawk Abbey swoops down from the black night sky. "Awwk! Awwk!" she squawks. She flaps her wings and dive-bombs you and Kip.

"Duck!" you shout to Kip.

"Hawk!" Abbey screeches from above. Then she swoops down on you again.

You hear the flapping of her giant wings as she flies by your head and digs her sharp claws into your skull. You scream out in pain!

Without stopping she turns in mid-air and attacks Kip with the same skull-cracking force.

"Abbey! Abbey! It's me!" Kip pleads. "Don't do this!" Abbey circles, ready for another attack.

"Ring the bell!" you shout to Kip. "Maybe the noise will scare her away!"

Kip reaches his hand up for the side of the bell. His fingers just miss it as Abbey the Nighthawk flies between the bell and his hand. She opens her mouth and closes it tightly on the back of his shirt. With Kip dangling from her teeth, she swoops down over you and grips your shirt with her hawk claws.

Get carried away to PAGE 43.

Your coin landed on heads, so HEADS it is. You push the button. The glass wall slides open to a low-ceilinged room. A sign above the door warns you to WATCH YOUR HEAD.

You duck down slightly as you enter a room with rows and rows of shelves lined with *heads* from medieval times! There are women's heads, men's heads, and even weird heads of beasts.

"How strange!" Abbey gasps.

"They look so real," Kip says. He's pretty scared.

"They're just mannequin heads." You laugh a little nervously. "Probably the museum uses them in exhibits to model old hats and stuff."

"You might be right," Abbey says as she walks along one of the rows of heads. She stops in front of one of them. She smiles. It looks like the head of a queen. "Now here's something I could get into. Look at the diamonds on that tiara. I wouldn't mind modelling that myself!"

What you see next makes your eyes bulge.

"Abbey!" you splutter. "What happened?"

Follow Abbey's head to PAGE 79.

104

"It's no use," Abbey complains breathlessly after running first one way and then the other. "The cottage is never where it seems to be. I'm too tired to run any more."

"So am I," Kip says, collapsing on the ground next to his sister. "We'll just have to take our chances with the Knight in Screaming Armour. I need some sleep."

"No! We can't sleep!" you say. "I'm tired too, but if we sleep, the Evil Knight will destroy us."

Everything is quiet now. You fight sleep. Abbey and Kip fight it too, but you can see they are losing. They both fall into a deep sleep.

Only you are awake to stand guard. A cloud rolls over the moon. It's impossible to see anything. Behind you a crackling of underbrush signals a footstep.

"Who goes there?" you shout into the darkness.

No answer.

The footsteps crush the brush again. You hear breathing. Closer. Closer. Slowly, you reach a hand out in front of you. In total darkness your fingers touch . . . metal!

Go to PAGE 37.

The loud *SLAM* of the door startles you. You jump sixty centimetres into the air. When you come back down, the floor beneath you opens up.

"A trapdoooooooor!" you exclaim. The three of you plunge downwards. It seems like you're falling for a while. Then your luck changes. You land on a soft bed covered with brown cloth.

"Whew!" you sigh, catching your breath. "I don't know where we are. But am I glad to be away from that old man. I can't explain it, but his voice really gave me the creeps!"

"I keep telling Abbey the same thing," Kip teases. "I can't explain it, but her face really gives me the creeps."

"Don't push your luck, Kip," Abbey warns, and she whacks him with a piece of brown cloth.

"What are these, anyway?" Kip asks. He lifts up the coarse brown sheet that just hit his face.

"They're monks' robes!" Abbey answers. "See?" She puts one on over her head. She looks just like a monk in a film.

"Cool!" You and Kip try them on too, just for fun. "What are they doing in this old man's basement?"

"Shhhh!" Abbey hushes you. "Listen!"

The sound of low chanting comes from somewhere above you. "Do you think it's the Knight in Screaming Armour?" you ask. "It sounds more like singing than moaning."

Tiptoe to PAGE 123.

106

You gasp. All around you, cages hold hideous mutant faces and monstrous shapes. Something about them looks strangely familiar too. Then you realize—the Evil Knight has gathered together all of the most terrifying creatures FROM YOUR OWN WORST NIGHTMARES!

To the right—there behind those bars—looms a hulking purple mound of slime. It has two enormous, watery, yellow eyes and it's sweating snails! They pop out of its skin and crawl towards you! "Oh, gross!" you hear yourself say.

Just to your left is the dark and silent outline of an executioner with a broad, flat axe. Without thinking, you grab your neck. Your eyes grow wider.

There are vampire bats, tarantulas and a howling werewolf with mucus-slimed fur. Next to the werewolf, cages of scraggly-haired, wart-covered old women reach for you through slime-covered bars.

Scaly-skinned dragons breathe fire at your face when you look in their direction. Hissing vipers hang down from the ceiling and brush against your ears. One wriggling snake drops on to your shoulder.

Quick, turn to PAGE 10.

The clock. You've got to use the clock. But how? No use trying to reverse time while you're under the spell of the Keeper of All Times. Then you notice something strange. Your eyes are getting watery but you can still see it. The old woman is aging too! She's hideously old. Older than you.

You get an idea. Maybe—if you push the clock hands forward—maybe she'll die first! It's risky. But right now it seems to be your only shot.

Your shaking old hand moves slowly against the hands of the clock. They move forward minute by minute. You are all aging, but the old woman is aging faster. One more minute to go and she will fall to nothingness.

"No!" the woman cries. "No! I'm cracking . . ."

10 . . . 9 . . . 8 . . . 7 . . . 6 . . . 5 seconds left. You, Abbey and Kip lean on each other's tired old bones and watch the wafer-thin-skinned woman withering away. You don't have the strength to look away. 4 . . . 3 . . . 2 . . . 1 second to go. GONE! It's over! The woman is nothing more than a paper-thin piece of parchment on the floor! You have destroyed one more evil force. For the old woman it's

THE END.

But for you, there's more to come on PAGE 6.

You know you should run. But for some reason your legs won't move. "We're stuck!" you yell. "Stuck!" You try to move your feet, but they are rooted to the ground. In fact, they are in the ground!

Kip and Abbey can't move either. Their feet are just as rooted as yours. And both of their bodies have started to turn green. They're getting thinner too. Very, very thin. So are you! Old Mr Triple-Decker is casting his favourite spell. He's mumbling some gibberish over there in the corner.

You have become the latest addition to his garden. You look out from your petal-framed face and see the petunias and snapdragons you passed on your way in. Funny. Now you notice they have faces.

"He got you too, I see," a purple petunia rooted next to you says. "No one knows the evil he sows!"

"Curses, soiled again!" a zinnia teases.

"He got all of us," Abbey sighs from beneath her rose-petalled bonnet. "But at least *I'm* a rose!"

Looks like you're grounded this time. But life in a wizard's garden can't be all bad. Who knows? It might even grow on you.

THE END

You turn the hands on the hot-pink clock forward—a little bit too far, by accident. Immediately you feel your joints stiffening. "Hmm, that's strange," you say. And then you hack a big cough.

"What's that you say, Sonny?" a squeaky voice says. It's Kip! But he looks grotesque! He's hunched over and leans closer as he cups his right ear with one hand. "Speak up there, youngster!" he squeaks. He's getting older and older before your very eyes.

"Who are you calling a youngster there, Grandpa?" Abbey cackles. Her face is a mess of wrinkles. You see them forming on her face like worms, doubling and tripling themselves. She looks older than your grandmother. Whoops! Make that your great-grandmother!

"Stop the clock before it's too late!" Kip screeches in an ancient-sounding voice. Your hands are wrinkled and gnarled now. Your fingers can hardly move over the clock face. You sneeze and when you do, an old woman appears before you. It's like she came out of your nose!

"Who summons me with a sneeze?" demands the raggedy old woman. "Was it you, old man?" she asks, whirling round and pointing a crooked, bony finger at you.

Turn to PAGE 18.

110

You pull down on the rotten rope. It breaks off in your hands!

"No bell tolls for us! No bell tolls for us! No bell tolls for us!" The ghostly, hooded robed monks chant solemnly. They've made it to the bell tower where you are!

Abbey and Kip reach their hands out to you. *"Join us,"* they drone. *"Be one with us. No bell tolls for us. No bell tolls for us."*

"Abbey! Kip!" you plead with them. "Don't fade! Don't fade!"

It's no use. Your cousins' faces are getting fainter and fainter. The chanting of the monks echoes in your ears. *"No bell tolls for us. No bell tolls for us. No bell tolls for us."*

You know you have to escape from here before it's too late.

Race to PAGE 88.

The Knight in Screaming Armour lies silent at your feet! You can't believe it. It's almost too good to be true. But it is!

You turn to the Sorceress and lift your battleaxe in a salute to her.

Then, *THWACK*! to your armoured back. A powerful blow crushes you to your knees. It sends vibrations ringing through your armour and every one of your bones.

The Evil Knight has not finished with you yet.

The armour you're wearing is very heavy. But you manage to lift yourself back to your feet. You raise your battleaxe again and wait for the chance to move in.

"WELCOME TO YOUR KNIGHT-MARE!" the Evil Knight bellows at you.

But you've heard that before. If he thinks he's going to scare you away, he's got another thing coming. And, in fact, he does have another thing coming: the sharpened blade of your battleaxe!

It's now or never. While he's still laughing his wicked laugh, you set your feet, swing round in a full circle, and release the battleaxe like a Frisbee. Almost in slow motion, it travels towards his face. It smashes into him in a burst of smoke.

See through the vapours on PAGE 136.

112

When you glance around you are shocked to see that you are back in your own garage! Everything is familiar. Two giant crates stand in front of you. One is labelled: EVIL KNIGHT. The other one says: GOOD KNIGHT.

The garage isn't the only thing that's familiar. Everything you're saying and hearing is strangely familiar, too! At least for a moment. Then it all starts to seem normal again . . .

"Which one should we open?" you say nervously.

"Neither!" Kip replies. He seems terrified.

Maybe a little *too* terrified. You're not sure you believe all this curse stuff. Maybe it's all a big trick. Kip and Abbey could have got someone to shout and shake the crate around. Who's really in that Evil Knight crate, anyway? you wonder.

Then again. Those screams do sound pretty spooky!

Maybe you should play it safe and open the crate marked GOOD KNIGHT. A suit of armour could come in handy if there *is* a crazy curse.

If you open the crate marked GOOD KNIGHT, *turn to PAGE 33.*

If you open the crate marked EVIL KNIGHT, *turn to PAGE 49.*

The garage door swings up and out of your way.

Dark was never as dark as this. Monsters seem to lurk in every corner. Familiar forms look strange. The beam of your torch cuts past the frightful shadowy figures to the two crates. They stand like tombstones in the middle of the garage. Except that one of them is vibrating. Shaking back and forth.

The light reflects off a label on one of the crates. The one with the curse on it. Then you notice another handwritten label near the top of each crate. One says: EVIL KNIGHT. The other reads: GOOD KNIGHT.

"Which one should we open?" you say nervously.

"Neither!" Kip replies. He seems terrified.

Maybe a little *too* terrified. You're not sure you believe all this curse stuff. Maybe it's all a big trick. Kip and Abbey could have got someone to shout and shake the crate around. Who's really in that Evil Knight crate, anyway? you wonder.

Then again. Those screams do sound pretty spooky!

Maybe you should play it safe and open the crate marked GOOD KNIGHT. A suit of armour could come in handy if there *is* a crazy curse.

If you open the crate marked GOOD KNIGHT, *turn to PAGE 33.*

If you open the crate marked EVIL KNIGHT, *turn to PAGE 49.*

114

You look at Abbey and are amazed to see her boldly batting at some hanging snakes. She's pretty brave, you think.

"Get away from my hair!" she yells as she knocks another snake to the ground. Then she misses one. It drops on to her shoulder and starts to wrap itself round her head!

"Aaahh!" Abbey cries. "Help me!" She falls to the floor, pulling at the snake. "Help!" she screams again. "Save me!"

Kip tries to be brave. He runs to help his sister. In his rush, he trips into an open-mouthed steel trap. His left leg is grabbed by the jagged metal teeth of the trap. "Help!" Kip cries. He can't get free to help Abbey. He can't even help himself.

It's all up to you now. Only *you* have a chance of earning the right to wear the armour of the Good Knight.

Turn to PAGE 126.

The huge, black bird takes a sudden turn to the left. "Help!" you yell. You tumble off the bird's back.

"Help!" Kip cries as he too is thrown from the feathered back of the bird.

Luckily, the bird is flying low to the ground. Unluckily, the ground isn't ground at all. It's water!

SPLASH! You plunge into freezing cold water.

The bird screeches as it flies away.

"Sink or swim! Sink or swim! Sink or swim!" chant the voices of three withered old women standing on a nearby shore. And then a crashing wave sends you down into the deep.

If you can swim, turn to PAGE 45.
If you don't know how to swim, turn to PAGE 122.

116

It's no use trying to find your way out of the mess of hedges surrounding you.

"We'll have to break through," you decide. "It's our only choice."

"Okay, but I'd better not get a scratch!" Abbey warns. "I've worked too hard for this beautiful complexion."

The three of you turn your backs to the high, thick hedge. "On the count of three we ram it!" you say. You link arms. "One, two, three!" you count. All together you throw yourselves backwards against the towering green wall. You fall through, landing flat on your backs on the other side.

"Hooray!" Kip cheers. "We did it!"

Before you and Abbey can add your own cheers, thousands of little animals tumble out of the hedge and cover you! Their fur is thick and coarse like spines.

"Ooooooooh! I hate dirty critters!" Abbey exclaims. "Get out of my hair!"

"Hedgehogs!" you cry. "They're holding us down."

Quick, turn to PAGE 94.

You're alone and still falling. It began as a fast fall. But now it's more like you're floating gently. You look up and barely see the black nighthawk. Kip managed to stay on the bird. Will you ever see Kip and Abbey again?

Below, you see emerald-green grass. It's getting closer and closer. You can tell your landing isn't going to be deadly, though. The grass will make a soft cushion for your fall.

You float down, settling at last on a moss-covered knoll—right in front of a familiar cottage!

The front door opens. A voice whispers, "Come in. You are so good to visit me."

You have no choice, turn to PAGE 77.

"Show your face, Evil Knight!" You nervously challenge the master of this evil museum again.

"Choose your weapon. Choose your weapon," chants the scraggliest of all the caged old women. She points a bony finger to a platform where a battleaxe, a gleaming sword, a jousting lance and a dagger are on display.

"Hmmm," you say. "I wonder why I didn't see that there before?" You step closer to the platform to get a better look.

As you reach across to take hold of the battleaxe, all the weapons vanish! Shining like a hundred mirrors, a gleaming silver suit of armour appears in their place.

Could it be? you think. Could it be the armour of the Good Knight at last?

As you step forward to touch the armour, it disappears into thin air.

Then, *WHAM!* An iron cage crashes down around you!

Sorry—it's not the armour of the Good Knight at last. But it is your last good night.

THE END

Kip and Abbey follow you through the hole in the back of the crate. When all three of you are through, something slams shut behind you. You turn to look, and the crate has disappeared! All you see around you are hills. Soft, green, rolling hills.

"It's so beautiful," you say. "It's a whole new world." You rub your eyes, but it doesn't go away.

"It's OUR world!" Abbey exclaims. "We're back in England!"

"It's exactly where the Evil Knight wants us to be," Kip says softly. "England. The land of the Saxtons. England."

"Who cares?" Abbey says. "We're home!"

"Don't look so happy," Kip warns. "The Evil Knight wants to destroy us. We may be home for good! Or should I say, for evil?"

You gaze around you stunned. There's no way to explain what's just happened to you. Hundreds of sheep are grazing on a nearby hill. One wild-looking ram glances up at you. Your heart jumps.

"His eyes are glowing!" you cry out.

Your pulse starts to race. The horned head of the ram morphs into the armoured head of the Evil Knight! He lowers his head and paws the ground. Steam pours through the grille on his helmet.

"He's going to ram us!" you cry. "Run for your lives!"

Run to PAGE 97.

"You really had us going there," Kip says as he and Abbey follow you into the house.

"I told you not to tell those stupid stories about the Knight in Screaming Armour," Abbey scolds her brother. "You gave our cousin nightmares!"

After a good group laugh, the three of you head back to bed. When you hang your gown over your desk chair you notice little prickly leaves stuck to it.

"Huh?" you say. Where did those leaves come from? you wonder. There aren't any thorn bushes like that around here. Maybe it wasn't a dream at all!

You climb into bed and pull your covers up to your chin. Your eyes are getting tired. You listen for a few seconds to hear if any noises are coming from the garage. Nothing.

Not this time. But before? *Hmmmmm*, you think as your eyes finally close. *Maybe. Oh well.* "Good-night," you say to no one in particular.

"Evil Knight," replies a deep voice next to you on your pillow. You feel a gust of hot air on your face.

THE END

When the rumbling of the avalanche has finished, you brush the dust off your face and glance round.

In the light of the full moon you see a trench in the middle of the hill. "It worked!" you shout. "The avalanche has cleared a path!"

"And look what I've found," Kip says. He holds up a shiny metal key. "It was right here under this rock."

"Kip, you're a genius!" you say again happily.

Turn to PAGE 134.

You sink into the deep, cold water. Deeper and deeper. Your lungs are about to burst from holding your breath so long. At last you sink to the bottom of this lake and land at the mouth of an underwater cave.

You motion to Kip and thrash for the opening. He's right behind you.

You flail into the cave, through a tunnel and up a channel to air!

"Pfwah!" You exhale. "Huuup!" You gulp in the fresh air. Kip does the same until both of you are breathing normally again.

"Come in," a familiar voice welcomes you. "We've been waiting for you."

You can't quite place it. Where do you know that voice from? *Hmmmmmmm.* "*We*'ve been waiting for you . . ."

Turn to PAGE 56.

You see stone steps in the corner of the basement.

"We'd better see what's up there," you whisper. You lead the way up the stone steps. Medieval paintings line the walls. Carved angels hover near the arched ceiling. "It's like a castle," you say.

"It's a monastery!" Abbey corrects you. "Monks probably used to live here centuries ago."

"Then who's that chanting in the next room?" Kip gulps. The chanting grows louder and louder as you enter a large dining-room. Long benches are filled with robed figures bent over a narrow wooden table. The figures keep their hooded heads bowed. They chant over their meal.

"There's no food on the table!" Kip whispers loudly.

All the figures turn round at once.

"Oh!" Abbey lets out a startled cry.

The robes are empty! Where their faces should be, there's empty space! They're ghosts!

You make a break for the stairs. But you're all alone when you get there.

Find out why on PAGE 135.

You may be climbing on pieces of people, but as rocks, they're not going to hurt you—or you, them, for that matter.

Kip and Abbey are probably fine. Maybe they just can't hear you.

If they are turning to stone, they're not going anywhere, are they? And you're not sure what you could do to help them, anyway.

You decide to keep climbing the last little bit up the slope. You'll grab that shining object—whatever it is—while you've got the chance. You're almost there.

The rock you're standing on is really unstable. You have to do a real balancing act to keep from crashing down on the rocks below. Slowly, carefully, you reach for the silver object. It's long and shiny.

When you've got a hold of it, you try to lift it up. But it lifts you up! Up into the air. The shiny thing is a metal finger that's attached to a metal hand that's attached to ... THE KNIGHT IN SCREAMING ARMOUR!

Meet your doom on PAGE 66.

The speeding black nighthawk doesn't hear you. It just keeps flying. The mountainside approaches. *CRASH!*

Purple stars flutter before your eyes. Your toes feel numb. Darkness surrounds you. You feel your own arm just to see if you're alive. "I am alive!" you shout happily.

"You call this living?" Abbey's voice says.

"Abbey!" you and Kip both say. "It's you! What happened?"

"We crashed and now we're crushed! That's what happened."

Abbey's right. The crash seemed to break the spell. Now you're crushed together inside the Evil Knight's crate! Back in your garage! In America! Home!

"It started when we entered the crate," Kip says groggily. "A secret door, another world and time . . . and . . ."

". . . and the worst night of my life! Aawwk!" Abbey squawks. She pushes on the door of the crate. You bang on it. Kip throws his weight against it. It won't open.

"AAAaaaaaahh! Aaaaah!" It's your scream coming from inside the crate. But you can scream all you want, no one's going to let you out. They've heard it all before. Those screams inside that crate. It's just the Curse of the Knight in Screaming Armour. A curse that never comes to an

END.

126

Over your cousins' cries for help, the scraggly old women in cages cackle, "Fight the evil! Earn the armour!"

Bats baring vampire fangs fly down at you from above. You flail your arms at them. The fire of the dragons' breath reaches for you with its flaming fingers. You shield your eyes. You take a deep breath and move towards the steel trap holding Kip's leg.

Before your hand gets close enough to try to free him, a gust of smoke fills the room. Huge puffs of black smoke burn your eyes. "I can't see a thing!" you shout.

You put your hands out in front of you and feel something smooth and metallic. A suit of armour!

You rub the smoke from your eyes and squint. "Yes!" you shout. "It's the armour of the Good Knight!"

You try to open the armour to put it on. It's no use. No amount of tugging will get you into the suit. You haven't earned the right to wear it yet.

"Grab the battleaxe!" Kip cries.

The armour holds a gleaming battleaxe in its glove.

"Please save us," Abbey pleads as she pulls at her snakeskin necklace.

You yank the battleaxe from the steel-gloved hand of the suit of armour. It pulls free!

Go to PAGE 129.

Kip and Abbey burst through the door.

"What's happening in here?" Abbey shouts.

"We heard terrible screams!" Kip adds. "Are you okay?"

You sit up. That's right. You sit up and push the covers aside. You're in BED! Back at HOME! At last!

"It was the Knight in Screaming Armour. We had an awesome battle and I killed him!" you exclaim proudly. "I broke the curse and brought us home!"

"What are you talking about?" Kip asks. "The Knight in Screaming *what*? Oh, you mean that crazy story my grandfather used to tell? How did you know about that?"

"Kip! Abbey!" you shout. "You have to remember! The Evil Knight was going to destroy all that was good 'unless a brave and noble Saxton could defeat it'. Remember? We fought the Evil Knight!"

"You? Battled against a knight?" Abbey says as she flicks her hair. "In your dreams!"

But it wasn't in your dreams. And the proof is on your bedroom floor at Abbey's feet: a small crumpled-up scrap of metal. You almost didn't notice it. Except that it's steaming.

Now you know that this story has come to a happy

END.

"COME FORWARD!" the Evil Knight repeats from the darkness behind the door. His voice works some evil magic on you. You see black and white spirals spinning before your eyes. You struggle to look away, but you can't. "COME FORWARD! COME FORWARD!" he booms. You are hypnotized by his command.

"No!" Abbey cries. "Cover your ears! Don't listen to him! Don't go in there! I *command* you!"

But still your feet shuffle forward.

You get a funny feeling as you pass through the doorway. Somehow, you know this room isn't on the official map of the Medieval Museum.

But still, you've just got to see what's in there!

"Stop!" Kip yells as you enter the dark room. "It could be a torture chamber, or filled with hungry beasts! Come back!"

Poor Kip, he could never understand . . .

Follow your feet into the darkness on PAGE 90.

All the creatures in the cages are pressed against the bars heckling. The purple one spits snails at you. They crunch under your feet as you walk. The werewolf snarls through his drool. It takes all of your strength to lift the enormous battleaxe.

Then you swing it.

It crashes down on the werewolf's cage like a tonne of bricks. There's an explosion. A burst of smoke. And when it all clears, the beast has gone!

You swing the axe again. This time at the dragons. They explode too! One by one they vanish—the bats, the vipers, the wretched hecklers, even the steel trap holding Kip's leg. They all go up in puffs of smoke.

"You've done it!" Abbey shouts happily. "You saved us!"

"Good work, cousin!" Kip adds, patting you on the back. Each pat sends a metal ringing through your ears. You're staring out at your cousins through a metal face mask!

"Hey!" you cry out. "Hey! Hey! Hey!" your voice echoes back. Suddenly, you realize you're not the same kid you were a minute ago. You have confronted all your fears and won! Your bravery has earned you the right to wear the armour of the Good Knight!

But it's not THE END, the Evil Knight is waiting for you on PAGE 80.

130

It's a Dorm of Doom, and you're the only student. A ghastly light shines from somewhere above you. The yellow glow reveals a throne. On the throne is a woman. She smiles. "Are you the mighty Saxton who will fight for right?" she asks.

"Me? I-I-I'm j-j-j-just a k-k-kid," you stammer.

"PUT ON THE ARMOUR!" the woman bellows.

You feel something hard against your back. You turn and come face to face with a shining suit of silver armour. You gasp. One steely-gloved hand holds a battleaxe. The other hand holds a shield engraved with the Saxton family crest.

Magically, the armour pops open. You don't know what else to do, so you step in. It closes in around you.

You feel taller and stronger than you've ever felt before. The battleaxe feels like a feather in your armoured, gloved hand. You look out from the silver face mask. The woman on the throne starts to laugh.

"Yes, yes," she cackles. "That is the way Sir Edmund looked when he got what he deserved. And I'm the one who GAVE IT TO HIM! I'm the SORCERESS!"

If you feel ready for battle, turn to PAGE 80.

If you don't think you're ready, turn to PAGE 64.

The hanging light bulb starts to spin. Kip struggles to lift his sister to her feet. He looks really scared now. It's going to be up to you to do something. But what? Should you open the Evil Knight's crate and confront the enemy—whatever it is? Maybe it's all just a practical joke. You wouldn't put it past Kip, would you?

Then again, maybe there really *is* a curse. If there is, maybe whatever's in the crate marked GOOD KNIGHT could help you. You'd better open one of them. Which will it be?

If you open the crate marked EVIL KNIGHT, turn to PAGE 49.

If you open the crate marked GOOD KNIGHT, turn to PAGE 38.

132

"Ouch!" Abbey cries. She breaks herself free from the prickly bush. You can't help laughing. Abbey's a human pincushion! She has little prickly leaves stuck all over her.

"OUCH!" you and Kip say together as you fall out of the bushes. You find yourselves looking like two porcupines too.

You hear giggles. And they're not Abbey's. You glance over your shoulder and see something you never imagined you'd see.

Two miniature men are laughing and rolling on the ground. Each man is about the size of a football. They laugh and smack their knees and point at you.

"Pixies!" Kip cries.

"Pixies?" you say. "You've got to be kidding me!"

The little men disappear for a minute. They resurface in the bushes close by.

"This way out!" one giggles, pointing to the left.

"No, this way out!" says the other, pointing to the right. Which one can you trust?

Follow the pixie pointing to the left on PAGE 32.

Follow the pixie pointing to the right on PAGE 100.

You peer closer at the hand sticking up out of the rocks. It's only made of stone! That's when you notice that the rock you're sitting on has a face!

"Aaaah!" you yell. The stone face is frozen in an expression of pain. You move to another rock. But as you look around, ALL of the broken rocks are shaped like PEOPLE! BROKEN PIECES OF PEOPLE!

"Abbey! Kip!" you cry. But there's no answer.

You can't see them from where you are without losing your balance. What if they're turning into stone or something! You think. You call out again. But again, there's no reply.

What's going on? Maybe they just can't hear you from down below. But maybe you should climb back down and check on them. Just to be safe.

If you keep climbing for the shimmering object, turn to PAGE 124.

If you scramble back down the mountain to help your cousins, turn to PAGE 35.

134

The three of you make your way up the path. All the way up and over the top of the hill. Off in the distance, you see a cottage.

"It's that cottage again," you say. Then you have an idea. "The key! Maybe it fits the door to that cottage!"

After walking on all those rocking rocks, the trip to the cottage is easy. No pixies change your path. No sheep stampede. And so far there's no Evil Knight in sight.

"Hurry!" you call to Kip and Abbey. You move quickly and quietly along the dirt road to the cottage.

When you are a few metres from it, you stop to look at the cottage more carefully. It's a small, two-storey, white building with a thatched roof. A bed of petunias and snapdragons lines the curved stone walkway leading to the heavy wooden door.

"I wonder who lives here?" Abbey asks. "It's quite stylish in an old-fashioned way."

She peeks in the windows. "It's too dark in there," she whispers. "I can't see a thing!"

You knock on the door. There's no answer. You knock harder. Still no answer.

"Try the key," Kip suggests.

You put the silver key in the lock and try to twist your hand.

Turn to PAGE 39.

When you get to the stone steps, you look back for Abbey and Kip. But they're not there.

Then you see them. They're walking over towards the table. What are they doing? "Come on, you two! This way!" you shout. But it's too late. Their faces are already starting to fade!

The chanting grows louder. Now you can hear what they're saying. *"No bell tolls for us. No bell tolls for us,"* they chant.

Find out what it means on PAGE 41.

136

"AAAaaaahhhh!" the Evil Knight screams again. But this time his screams fade slowly away. Through the smoke you see the heap of black armour shrivel up and turn into . . . into . . . a ball of tin foil on the floor.

From the throne in the corner, the Sorceress cries out, "No! No! All spells are broken! All spells are broken!"

You watch in amazement as her throne disappears. Her Sorceress robes turn to rags. Her face grows older and older even as you watch. The evil creatures round you shrivel and vanish.

The Sorceress is nothing more now than a bent and withered old woman. The iron gate has gone. The darkness in the dungeon starts to lift.

Then, you hear pounding on the door behind you.

POUND! POUND! POUND! What could it possibly be now?

Turn to PAGE 127 to find out!

Give Yourself Goosebumps

A scary new series from R.L. Stine – where *you* decide what happens!

Choose from over 20 scary endings!

Goosebumps

R.L.Stine

Reader beware, you're in for a scare!

These terrifying tales will send shivers up your spine:

Goosebumps

Reader beware – here's THREE TIMES the scare!

Look out for these bumper GOOSEBUMPS editions. With three spine-tingling stories by R.L. Stine in each book, get ready for three times the thrill … three times the scare … three times the GOOSEBUMPS!